Into the Darkness

Jo Wilkinson

TSL Publications

First published in Great Britain in 2022
By TSL Publications, Rickmansworth

Copyright © 2022 Jo Wilkinson

Cover image: Jo Wilkinson

ISBN /978-1-914245-89-3

1

Vince stood inert on the stairway. Voices reverberated as all hell broke forth above. Firearms cracked their accustomed, deadly song. They waited, ready to spring the trap should any escape. Footsteps! He nodded to his companion across the hallway. Feet emerged, followed by legs, pattering swift and silent. His automatic sprang into action. Blood splattered the walls. Other feet followed. His hand froze on the trigger as the familiar face appeared.

"No!" he yelled turning to his companion in arms. In slow motion he saw the smile, the finger on the trigger, the bullets race, the face smashed, exploding to bloody pulp in a rain of bullets as he stood splattered by crimson rain.

"No! no!" he screamed, but the darkness did not hear.

Hands were shaking him. A face appeared, dim in the moonlight. "Wake up! Wake up!" it urged as he struggled against the darkness.

"I'm OK ... just a bad dream ..." he lied.

"Pretty awful dream to have you yelling like that! Wanna talk about it?"

"No, it's nothing, nothing ..." More faces, young, concerned, glancing back and forth. What did they know? "I'm alright I tell you!" The edge to his voice made them wary. They withdrew.

Alone again in the darkness, Vince sought control. It was always like this, always, because it was no dream. Jase was dead, and nothing he could do would bring him back. He'd tried to warn him, but he hadn't listened. Now the face was still and shattered, the body cremated or thrown into a mass grave, as were all anti-government rebels ...

It had been the catalyst for Vince's own rebellion... He thought of Chad, of Rat and his former comrades, of life in the wilderness, of revenge ... Now they were all left behind save the two who travelled with him, even the repressive world government was gone. *We are free now,* he told himself. Jase would want that. Was Jase like Chad he wondered? He'd glimpsed Chad, Chad who'd engineered their exodus from Special Forces, who'd forged them into a deadly vigilante group, Chad whose body lay beneath the hills somewhere ... The vision had been veiled, eclipsed by the radiance of a being of absolute power. A being who'd given him a second chance due Chad's pleading, but it was hard to let go of the hate. The dreams made it worse.

Morning dawned clear and bright, driving entangling cobwebs of night away. Someone was singing. Vince rolled up his blanket, enticed by the smell of breakfast. It was one of the perks of joining "the innocents" as he'd inwardly dubbed them. They knew so little of life, of evil – that was why he'd come, that and the prospect of women. He wondered if the messenger had it right, ten women to every man they'd said. From what he'd heard of the war it was a wonder anyone survived, but that had been mostly in the Middle East. China was virtually untouched – by war at least. The men had gone to fight and never returned. Here in the States it was different, there'd been few women in the wilderness ... It had been a long, long time since he'd had a woman ...

"Morning Vince," There was hesitation in John's smile, caused doubtless by last night's uproar.

Vince nodded his acknowledgement. He knew John wanted to help, but it was too much right now, the wound had reopened. Eyes glanced furtively in his direction, unsure what to do. He grasped the bowl Ellen thrust towards him, moving away rather than join the sitting throng.

"Best to leave him be when he's like this," Alex whispered. The youngsters were content to take Vince's old comrade's advice, only John continued to watch. He couldn't stand to see an animal in pain, much less a human being.

"Do you know what the dreams are?" he whispered. Alex shook his head. "None of us know much about Vince, except he was a damned sadistic bastard." That was little reassurance. John wondered what they'd got themselves into in taking Vince along. The "messenger" had assured them the government had fallen, its emissaries and all to take its trading chip destroyed, but perhaps he was wrong in his assumption that all those remaining were peaceful? It seemed a tiger strove within Vince, a beast lurking, yet to be aroused. As leader it was his job to keep an eye on things. He should have asked Rat about Vince as he had the others, but it had been a last-minute thing. It seemed a good idea at the time, but had he let a wolf among the lambs?

"Better get going." Vince turned with a snarl, irritated by how slow and careless they were. Wouldn't have lasted ten minutes in the "real world" he thought. Still, they'd been good to him, never pushed him to give up the secrets that rent his soul. He was torn between his intent to protect that innocence, yet at the same time irritated by it. Hidden away in their underground refuge, they'd seen nothing of the horror and devastation that had encircled the earth. Still, he was thankful to go with them now, to have a chance at a better life, if only he could overcome the hate, the smouldering anger …

They trudged on westward over strange new terrain. The Rockies were gone, replaced by devastation thinly camouflaged by nature's indomitable resurgence. There was little in the way of foraging. He'd not seen an animal in days … besides, his automatic lay somewhere back beneath the mountains. He remembered the feeling as the ground drained away, like sand, beneath him, the yawning abys, the overwhelming surge of light and Chad's heartfelt pleading.

He shook his head. That was over now – new beginnings! Perhaps they'd never make it … perhaps it was all a dream. Instinctively he rubbed his leg; the leg he thought would kill him, swollen, full of gangrene, now sound, strong, unmarked. Beings who could do that could surely lead them to a craft. He wondered if the sea itself were changed, perhaps like the mountains the Pacific it had dwindled. Perhaps the land masses had moved in those last colossal quakes. There was no way of knowing. It was impossible, as impossible as the way he walked unaided over rough terrain ...

He looked up. They were excited about something.

"The Pacific! I can see the ocean!" The lead figure was waving his arms, encouraging them to the top of the rise.

There it was, a vast expanse of blue sky and sea blending pale on the horizon. Gentle slopes led down towards it, a panorama of greens, patches of grey rock, and flaming colour – wildflowers blooming. The earth was slowly recovering its beauty. His companions burst into song.

Vince looked on sceptically. He felt awkward at such times. He didn't share their beliefs. Smith, they'd told him, had been visited by a celestial being, and they believed the same being was leading them. He didn't know what he believed. His world had been turned topsy-turvy the day of the quake. He dealt in facts, in reality ... Yet the being he'd encountered, whatever it was, had been real enough. Maybe one had visited Smith ... He cracked half a smile. It didn't matter. They were good kids. He felt a fatherly concern for them that they would not have suspected. He'd never had kids. He wasn't the kind of guy to settle long, even before. Now, in his late thirties, it seemed unlikely ... unless ...

John paused to fling an arm around Vince's shoulder bringing him into the throng. There was a time such an action would have met with stern rebuff, perhaps worse, but now ... Now as he looked at the sea of ecstatic faces Vince couldn't help but partake vicariously of the joy of youth.

They descended, scanning the area for any sign of a craft. There was none, but a dark irregular line appeared near the water's edge as if a cartographer had etched his boundary in the very earth itself. It remained puzzling, till, finally, they emerged at the shoreline. Though no more than fifty meters wide, a crevasse descended to infinite depths of darkness, cutting across their route to the ocean. It was as if the earth had cracked open like a shard of pottery to expose its inner heart. Looking down Vince felt his stomach turn.

"No way we're going to get across that one," he stated. John agreed.

"We'd better follow along south, no telling how far it might extend. We need to stay aligned to the south west currents." Vince nodded.

As they followed the canyon south, the tide rose, incoming waves converging to slide over the outer rim, descending like frail waterfalls, misting the depths of darkness below. Vince paused, transfixed by the bizarre beauty of it. The flow increased with the deepening tide, becoming, in places, a spectacle of mammoth proportions, dwarfing Niagara to a child's toy. How far did this extend Vince wondered? Magnificent as it was, it would make their westward journey difficult, if not impossible. They could be following a land fault, in which case they might have a long haul before them.

Evening was coming on. The fresh sea breeze was tainted by a pungent smell.

"Is it?" John whispered. Vince nodded.

"Something nasty up ahead. We could camp here and a couple of us go check it out."

"Sounds like a good idea. I can go."

"You?" Vince looked sceptical. "You've yet to see this kind of stuff. Leave it to me and one of my guys." John shook his head.

"Look, I know you think of me as totally wet behind the ears but it's my responsibility."

"Have it your own way, but don't blame me when you start puking, 'cos you will."

"At least there'll only be you to see," John cracked a grin. "Look, I may not have seen this stuff first-hand, but I have a pretty vivid imagination!"

"Upon your head be it."

Vince was right, John emptied his stomach several times as they passed through what had once been Reno. Jutting concrete and girders mocked trees and hillside in macabre parody, and everywhere the stench of death. Mutilated corpses bloomed among the debris, half eaten, half decayed, bloated and split by their internal devourers. John stopped suddenly, removing the vest covering his nose.

"What the hell is that?" Amidst a pile of bricks lay an extended, mottled, wing, like the remains of a giant bat. Vince examined the encumbering brickwork. A good kick confirmed his suspicions. This was what Chad had encountered. Grizzly remains clung in tendrils to the thick armour plating of the exoskeleton.

"The locusts?" John queried. Vince nodded, surprised. Did John know about the swarms?

"You could call it that. Chad said it looked more like a demon."

"That I can believe ... This guy Chad, he saw one?"

"Him and Brad were attacked by one."

"Sure wouldn't have liked to be in their shoes! Think there's any more left around?"

"No way of knowing. I sure as hell hope not. Haven't heard of any in months and this one's been dead a long while." John was edgy. Vince didn't blame him.

"Maybe we should head back," he suggested, "not much sense going further. Either we wade through all this or go around. It would be a long detour. We can decide in the morning." Vince clasped John's shoulder. He was looking decidedly green.

"Suppose you think I'm a real wimp," John ventured, brown eyes decidedly hang dog.

"Look man, there's no one can see stuff like that and not be affected."

"But you ... you hardly turned a hair."

"Well I'm used to it, military training and stuff, you get toughened."

"You were military?" Vince nodded, eyes hardening.

"World Government?"

"Yeah!" It came out with a hiss and John knew better than to probe further. The friendly arm was retrieved. They walked on in silence.

Back at camp Vince noticed John sitting a ways off with Ellen, digesting the day's events. The age-old remedy, a barrel load of alcohol and a good whore seemed hardly appropriate or indeed feasible. Vince ventured closer, he wasn't much for playing counsellor, but John had some hard decisions to make.

"Can I join you?" He wasn't asking, Vince never asked. John yielding to the inevitable, waved to the space beside him. "Make any decisions yet?"

John nodded. "We pass through."

"Going to be tough on these guys and what about Ellen?" Vince nodded at John's attendant wife, the only woman of the group.

"Yes, I know, but sooner or later they're going to need to come to terms with it."

Vince nodded. "You're right about that. Better here, Reno looks deserted. At least they're all dead by looks of it."

"You mean ...?"

"Don't know man. No one really knows what's out there. It's part of the reason I came."

"You came to protect us?" John looked surprised.

"Yeah, I figured there'd be stuff like this ... or worse ..." His words trailed off.

John glanced up making eye contact.

"Look we're not pussies you know. We don't hold with violence, but we'll fight to save our own. We've had our share of battles. Not everyone made it to the refuge, some stayed to fight so the rest could escape." His eyes misted over.

"Someone you were close to?"

"His father ..." whispered Ellen.

"Sorry man."

"I'm not the only one ... I want to be the kind of man he was,' John whispered. Vince squirmed. His habitual ridicule of naive ideologies seemed petty. John was young for a leader, couldn't be more than mid-twenties, and the responsibility weighed heavy on him, even Vince could see that. He bit back the sarcasm.

"You're a good son of a bitch, John," he muttered gruffly

instead. "It took courage to face that stuff ... You could have just let me and the boys check it out, but you faced your fears. That's the important thing. You have to face down fear! I did it with hate and anger. You ... you did it for them." He nodded at the chatting boys round the fire.

"Thanks." John looked up with half a grin. Vince moved off, uncomfortable with this unaccustomed role.

The mood was sombre as they moved on next morning, everyone aware what was ahead. Vince led, trying to pick the fastest, least traumatic routes – still it took its toll.

"Just keep going. Try not to look ..." John advised. Ellen was pasty faced and clinging like a leach. Bodies bloomed like lurid scarlet blots as they clambered over the debris. Stomachs were long empty, and a couple of guys were looking shaky. The pace dwindled.

"Get a move on. Don't want to be here come nightfall," Vince urged. That got them going. None the less, night fell before they were clear. They had a couple of heavy-duty torches, needed to find a way through, but gruesome in extreme when some new horror caught their spotlight glare. They continued till well clear of the city, their march illuminated by the reflective gleam of water as it once more reached high tide. A refreshing wind enwrapped their faces driving back the stench.

It was a subdued camp that night. No one got much sleep, despite utter exhaustion. John suggested a rest day, but pretty much all wanted to keep moving, to put as much space as possible between themselves and what they'd seen. Word spread about the weird bat like creature, further adding to the tension.

They kept a slower pace, the sound of the surf and intermittent bird song cleansing hearts and minds of what lay behind. Nature reasserted herself, the scars of devastation growing over with grass and ivy. Vince was concerned about food. While the baggage ponies and backpacks had carried ample supplies for their journey west, what if they needed to travel far south. What about the voyage itself? Food was scarce in this strange new world. Perhaps they should ration their provisions? Rat would have known how to forage, but Vince had always relied on rifles. Now he'd scarce seen an animal on their journey let alone one big enough to be worth pursuing.

In answer to his query John replied, "God will provide."

"Like the boat to cross the Pacific," Vince quipped. John shrugged. Sometimes Vince thought he'd been crazy to go with these guys. Maybe he should have stayed with Rat at the farm, at least it had a long-term food supply, but he'd been restless. He wasn't cut out to be a farmer, he needed action. Most of all he needed to keep running, to evade the shadows of his past. A hundred images flashed before his eyes. No matter how fast he ran they always pursued.

2

The chasm had been dwindling as they proceeded south. They'd discussed the possibility of building a bridge from fallen timber, but there was nothing to cross to, only the open water of the Pacific. Caught in the incoming tide they'd not last long.

Rounding a headland, a strange sight met their eyes. The coastline formed an extended bay. Ungirded by the dark line of the crevasse, instead it was littered with dark shapes protruding at angles from the water. On the furthest stretch, silhouetted against the evening light, stood the ruin of a city.

Pace increasing, they trundled closer, eager to figure it out. Could it be? Yes, yes it was! Ships, hundreds of craft, most smashed to pieces, but surely some, somewhere intact? John flashed a smile. Vince raised his hand dismissively.

"I ain't saying nothing!" he chuckled.

An iconic, wave swept, billboard, still sported remnants of its once flashing lights among the debris.

"Vegas ..." Vince breathed.

"What?" John questioned.

"It's Vegas, or what's left of it."

Half submerged, the skyscape was populated at intervals by smashed containers, liners and a myriad of smaller vessels lodged between half ruined towers of brick and concrete as if the sea had invaded then drained away, leaving craft and building eternally meshed. Part of the city lay beneath the waves, part tottering on the edge of the vast Pacific Ocean, but here at last was hope. Hope in the form of craft and a possibly navigable entry to the west.

The morning lent its taint of urgency, a longing to explore the possibilities. Descending to the shore they commenced their search over rock, twisted metal, wood and fiberglass.

"It's like the old pictures of elephant graveyards," John observed perusing the landscape.

"Yeah, only boats!" Vince acknowledged.

After several hours of dispirited searching they paused to eat. Breakfast had been a skimpy affair; they'd been in a hurry to explore. The initial euphoria had ebbed away as they encountered craft, after craft impossibly holed or half destroyed.

"It just takes one, just one!" John muttered between bites.

"Yeah, or maybe we'll need to rebuild somehow," Vince replied, recalling Rat's engineering skills and wishing he'd accompanied them. "Don't suppose any of your guys ..." John shook his head cutting him off.

"There's something else bothering me," Vince ventured. "You know what we ain't seen?" John raised an eyebrow in question. "We ain't seen a single body."

"Maybe the sea washed them off someplace, or the fish ... Can't say as I'm feeling sorry for that after last time ..." John cracked a grin.

"Some maybe, but look, the tide has left other stuff, why not bodies? Even given the tsunami, or whatever did this, you'd expect bodies, lots of them."

"What are you suggesting Vince?"

"I don't know, but ain't no fish or current can get a body out

12

from below deck, bones and all."

"You think someone buried them?"

"Maybe, maybe not. If there are survivors here, it would make sense to get rid of the bodies, death thrives on death."

"In either case we'd better keep looking."

"Any of you know about boats? We might need to make a fast get away if we find one."

"Well a couple of the guys did some sailing. Dave's dad had a boat, but that doesn't help much if we can't find a sound vessel. Why do you think we might need a fast get away?"

"Not all folks are as 'righteous' as you. We have food and pack animals, think about it!"

John preferred not to. He didn't want to see life in Vince's terms. Stuffing the last of his food in his mouth, he set about rounding up the boys.

A scuffling noise disturbed their afternoon search. Instantly alert, Vince leapt after the retreating figure.

"Come back! We mean you no harm!" John called, but Vince's hot pursuit precluded any thought of the fugitive to remain. Scrambling over the debris, he sank suddenly out of sight amid the wreckage of a container ship. A search proved fruitless.

"Damn! Lost him." Vince muttered.

"Why did you go off after him?" John shouted. "You scared him away!"

"What the hell do you think he was going to do? Hang around for a sermon on world peace?" His tone was cutting.

"Guess we'll never know now, will we? Maybe he could have helped us."

"Maybe he's off to set a bunch of thieves on us! Ever thought of that! Anyone left alive in a place like this is suspect." John paused. The thought had not occurred.

"Well whichever, it's too late now." Their search continued, fruitlessly. Vince kept ears and eyes open, but there was no further sign of life.

It was not till evening a second chance appeared. Vince slid into action, this time circling behind to cut off any retreat, while, at a signal from John, the others continued their activities. Checking the vicinity before making his presence known, Vince sprang, taking his victim by surprise. The man, middle-aged, strong and wiry, wriggled like an eel, but he was no match for Vince, who, pinning his arm behind him, marched him into the firelight.

"Can't you ease up a bit, Vince," John asked, catching the terror in the captive's eyes.

"Not unless you want him to take off again."

"It's like trying to hold a damned rattlesnake!" John moved closer.

"We don't want to hurt you. Just tell us who you are and what you are doing here. Are there others?"

"Just me! Only me!" he replied rapidly, voice tinged with Spanish.

"And your name?"

"They call me Waterman."

"They?" queried Vince. "Who's they?" His assessment that the man was lying, confirmed.

"No one. They're dead, all dead I swear you!" There was desperation in the dark, weather-seamed eyes. John tried a different tack.

"Waterman? Do you know about boats?"

"Of course, yes!" The figure ceased squirming for a moment. "If it's boats you want, I can help ... if you take me with you." The eyes grew wide.

"We need a boat, an ocean worthy vessel. Do you know of one?"

"Maybe ... depends."

"On what," Vince interjected.

"If you take me ... I know boats. You need someone who know the ocean. Is very dangerous! I sailed since boy."

"Navy?" Vince asked. No response.

"Merchant seaman?" John added in the ensuing silence.

"No ... maybe?" There was hesitation, confusion. The eyes went vacant for a moment. John and Vince exchanged glances.

"Look, maybe we can work something out. We need a good

seaman, but you must trust us. If Vince here lets you go will you promise not to run?" He nodded. Vince looked sceptical but released him, positioning himself for any escape attempt. Waterman appraised the situation.

"If help, how I know you don't leave me here?"

"I give you my word," John answered.

"Word?" Evidently that was not sufficient.

"Look!" Vince said, exasperated. "They're bloody saints! Can't you tell?"

"Saints? ..." Waterman appraised his captors, misunderstanding. A strange look came to his eyes. Despite their journeying, their clothes were new compared with his own tattered rags. The faces were young, fresh looking. A smile crossed his features. "Saints ..." He relaxed, crossing himself, then recalled Vince.

"You not saint!"

"Sure as hell I ain't, and if you so much as try to pull a fast one on these guys I'll hunt you down, and I'll give you one guess what my profession was." He had no need to say more. Though the uniform was long forsaken, the eyes and breadth of shoulder said it all. Waterman melted closer to John. Vince quenched John's denial of "sainthood".

"The guy's off his rocker," he hissed. "Play along."

"I know boat, good boat! No hole, engine good," Waterman pleaded. "But I need help free it. Small boat too. How far you want go?"

"China." The word fell like a bombshell.

"China! You crazy! Even on big boat you don't make it. El mar, the ocean, much storms, you sinking."

"God will help us. He's led us this far, led us to you," John replied stotically. "If you don't want to come I understand, we can trade something for your help – the ponies perhaps?" Waterman's expression changed from incredulity to horror.

"No ponies. We get out this place, go safe country. Canada maybe? South sea, fish dead. We stay close the land, maybe storms come."

"There's a huge canyon all the way up north."

Waterman looked puzzled. "Canyon?"

"Hole, like a big hole, can't cross. Only here we can get to the sea and the messenger said to go to China and that is where we are going, come what may." Waterman's face fell. "Well what do you think? Do you want to come with us or take the ponies?"

"Not China, not ponies."

"Well I guess we'll just keep looking, we're bound to find the boat sometime or other."

"No! You stop to look. I help you!" There was panic in his eyes Vince noted, there was more he wasn't telling them. Somewhere safe he'd said ...

Night was falling, the tide withdrawn. Waterman, fed and quieted by John, kept a wary eye on Vince, who was to accompany them. "Easier when the sea go out," he'd said. There were probably other reasons he preferred to wait for darkness Vince surmised, but so far John had been unable to prise anything of value from him. He seemed confused; his memory patchy at best. He was scared shitless of something, but were they figments of his imagination or did some tangible danger reside here? It was hard to tell.

"You don't leave me?" Waterman grasped John's arm.

"I won't leave you. We go together. I promise."

"Swear!" Waterman pointed to the cross at John's neck.

"I swear we won't cheat you. God is with us all, you've no need to fear."

"He not ... with me ..."

"I believe he has been. You're alive and he's led you to us, and we'll take care of you if you help us."

Vince rolled his eyes, but it seemed to work. Waterman's agitation calmed, and they set off. Circling the bay, he led them inland, approaching the water from the east.

"See, down there," he whispered, pointing into the shadows.

Vince took the torch from his bag. The beam barely shone forth when Waterman shrieked snatching it from his hand.

"What the …" Vince exploded, grabbing for it. Waterman was too quick, hurling it away into the darkness. The light glimmered for a moment then expired, the bulb smashed.

"Why you …" Vince seized him by his shirt, fist raised.

"Vince no! We need him!" John yelled, vainly grasping the threatening arm. "Please Vince, please! Listen to me."

"Why'd he do that! Why? You tell me!"

"Because he's scared," John whispered.

"Then he'd better tell us who or what he's scared of." Vince shook him like a rat.

"Please Vince," pleaded John. "Tell us Waterman. Why did you smash the torch?"

"They see us!"

"Who'll see? The people that are all dead?" Vince retorted sarcastically. John gave an imploring expression. Vince scowled.

"Tell us Waterman. Who's out there?"

"No puedo, no puedo, I can't. They gonna kill me like others."

"What others?"

"Keep me for fish. They gonna kill me. You too!"

"Look," Vince entered in, "if there's someone dangerous out there it's better we know. They won't find me so easy to kill."

"Have guns, knives. Killing what they do."

"But …" John hesitated. "You said no more guns Vince?"

"No more guns for us, no, but who's to say there are not some still out there. There must have been soldiers stationed here, and where there are soldiers there are guns."

"But the government troops are all dead?"

"Soldiers are not the only professional killers," Vince breathed.

"You mean like gangs?"

"Criminals, hit men, organised crime takes many forms. Prostitution had to be big here even under the, oh so moral, world government." Waterman was crying. Vince set him down.

"Por favor, que me no matan … no get me again," he whimpered. It was Vince that offered security.

"If they come near any of us, and that includes you, I'll kill the bastards," he hissed. "We'll see how good they are against Special Forces."

"You were ... Special Forces ..." John's voice trailed off. He knew of the atrocities.

"Not anymore. I left a good while ago." Vince's face grew hard, eyes steel sharp. "Now look, better they don't know we're here. Let's go down, take a look at this boat of yours."

"Come Waterman, No torches, no noise, OK? Show us where it is," John coaxed.

Hesitantly Waterman arose. Glancing several times at Vince, he scrambled downhill toward an expanse of water glistening in the moonlight.

Below them lay a conglomeration of craft, most in better condition than those they'd thus far seen.

"This way. Follow close." Waterman slipped into the lead traversing a narrow path down a steep muddy incline. He paused at the base indicating to wait. From scrawny bushes he pulled several wooden planks arranging them in a line, one after another.

"Step here," he warned, pointing to the planks. "It pull you in." He gestured to the muddy ground.

Warily, they negotiated the plank bridge. Going ahead, Waterman pulled them up on a rocky mound beside which lay what looked like a battered old rowboat.

"Looks a bit small?" John whispered to Vince. Waterman caught it.

"Not this boat. Come, wait. Sea come in, we go there." He waved toward a stretch of murky water. "When water over rock, we go." The rock in question lay half submerged, brushed by waves of the turning tide. "Have know water, when it come, when it go o ..." He made an expressive motion.

"So, it's all swamp here?"

"Swamp? What swamp? If you step, it pull you down. We be careful ... not get stuck."

"Looks like an enormous mudslide to me," John ventured.

"That's probably why the ships aren't so smashed up, it cushioned them."

"Yes, mud, but this pull you down."

"Quicksand." Vince spoke into the darkness. This wouldn't be as easy as they'd hoped.

"How can we push it off if the ground is quicksand?" John ventured.

"No mud by boat, rock. Like island. Little boat to get there. Strong water pulls, not good to swim. I keep boat here, safe place, no one get me here."

"You said they kept you for fish?" John whispered.

"Fish back, little fish. Here no more red water. I know where fish live, catch fish, baby fish, not catch many. Don't tell them where. Don't tell you. Only I know. They want I tell them, but I get away ... I get away ... hide here, find boat, big boat ... keep little boat here ... They don't see, don't come ..." His disjointed sentences dissolved into rapid Spanish, of which Vince could understand only a word here and there and John nothing.

Waves splashed over the rock. Vince looked up expectantly. Waterman nodded, clambering into the boat, gesturing them to follow. Hearts thudded as it sank lower in the water, but it didn't stick. Waterman, it seemed, knew his business. Taking the oars tucked beneath the seat he began to row quietly off into the shadows, strokes barely disturbing the surface. Moonlight danced on the waters hiding the danger beneath. His course was not straight Vince noticed, he seemed to be skirting something.

"Water deep here," he said by way of explanation. "Not stick." Such a trip would have been nerve-wracking enough in daylight but shrouded in darkness the tension was tangible. A cross loomed before them, a mast rising from the waters.

"That it?" John whispered.

"No," Waterman shook his head. "Too small. We need food and water, lots water! Maybe it rain, maybe not. You too many. Need a big boat. That motor not work. I take you to big boat, room for gas and water, and food." The placid sound of the oars continued for a while as another shape loomed.

They pulled alongside grasping a rotting rope ladder suspended from the deck above. John pulled on it gingerly.

"Will it take our weight?"

Waterman nodded. "I go lots of times ... I first." Stowing the oars, he swung onto the ladder, scrambling up with ease. John was slower in his ascent, easing himself over the rail before Vince followed.

The deck was tilted, but they were able to find their footing, following Waterman as he edged along.

"Careful," he hissed as he manoeuvred over piles of rope and debris towards a dark rectangle. The shape creaked and swung outward revealing a black hole within.

"Come, come!" He gestured them inside. Vince and John exchanged glances before following. There were scrambling noises. The door pounded shut behind them as a tiny glimmer of light appeared, followed by an increasing glow they recognised as an oil lamp.

"OK here. Don't see here. Come, look." He opened a door into a small room lined on either side by bunks. Books and clothes lay scattered on the floor, relics of former inhabitants. Bedding, now soiled and dirty, adorned the bunks, a ripped pillow deposited its tiny foam flotillas on a puddle of sea water. None of it mattered. If the vessel was sound, as Waterman assured them, there would be space enough for them all. John looked around counting bunks.

"Are there more cabins?" he asked.

"Three for sleep ..." Waterman held up three fingers and led them on to what seemed to be the captain's quarters, a galley and storage room. Vince whistled.

"She schooner ..." Waterman whispered the word as if questioning his translation. "She take people for holiday. Not boat for working, but beautiful." His hand slid affectionately over the peeling paintwork."

"A schooner?" Vince questioned. "Schooners are sail boats, right?"

"Yes, sails OK, tied up."

"Can you sail her though ... she's pretty big?"

"Need help. I teach how. She have engine, good engine, not broken."

"Why don't we just use the engine then," John put in.

"It would take too much fuel, wind is free. God knows where we'd get fuel these days," Vince stated. Waterman eyed him with new respect.

"You know boats?" he asked.

"No, but I know about survival."

"So how do we launch her?" John asked.

"The sea lift her, three, four men OK." John looked sceptical but Waterman seemed to know what he was doing.

"There's three of us?" Vince pointed out.

"No wood, no rope, no time to get, water go down."

"Tomorrow?"

"Yes, go early, get planks and rope. Then wait."

"Wait?"

"Wait in boat, water come in, water go out."

Mud smeared faces peered back at Vince, shoulders looped with scavenged lengths of rope and planks. It would be a long haul burdened down like this. Vince had requested he take his former colleagues, both for strength and covert abilities. John reluctantly stayed behind extending a futile search for food among the scattered wrecks. Someone had beaten them to it, that was clear.

It was hard negotiating the boards, loaded down. The rowboat also would need to take two trips. Vince waited with Alex while Waterman ferried the first batch.

Smart guy Waterman, he pondered, he'd got ropes to haul the planks up. No way that old ladder would take the weight. He hoped he'd got the rest figured out ... like Rat ... His thoughts drifted back as they often did. Rat was the only person he'd let in, apart from Chad of course, but then Chad knew his story ... He'd wanted Rat to come along, but he just couldn't get over Emmie, even knowing she was dead. He hoped Rat would find

21

someone in time to erase the memory. Hell, he hoped he'd find someone ...

Li Hua looked down. The shadow of death was on his face.

"Don't leave me! Please don't leave me!" she whispered. It was wrong to ask, but she felt so alone. He'd always been there and now with the children ... The eyes flickered a last farewell, the mouth twitched, an effort to smile, and he was gone. Si wan gone. Si wan who brought food to the village, who kept the soldiers away. Si wan who comforted her the first time ... He knew what it was like, from a young boy he knew. He'd learnt to block it out, to survive. He'd taught her the same, living a life of privilege, spoilt favourites of the elite. Pampered, hidden away in luxurious insecurity, knowing one misstep could mean their death.

His skin was still soft, pale like his name, "the swan" they'd called him. Best of all the Gaoshanzu dancers, slim, high cheek bones, his form would grace any woman. "Drag" they'd called it, but Si wan followed the ancestral tradition. No westerner could match the grace and beauty of their dancers. The governors used him to play tricks on visiting officials, old customs taking a new role. Si wan had been the protector of his village and hers ... Now he was gone, eaten up by the disease rampant in his trade, yet his translucent beauty remained even now.

Small, anxious faces peered through the window space. Now there were only children, the remains of their tribes, she and the children ... alone. Even the mountains were gone, swallowed in the last earthshattering quakes. Hualien, long reduced to ruin, half swallowed by sea, stalked by ghosts, held little of use, but the fields remained, the rice paddies, the fast-growing bamboo, coconut palms and bananas. God had not left them to starve. She too must live, for the children. Pour her life into their s...

The bunks were damp, and the smell of mound pervaded the cabin. He'd have preferred the deck, the open air, but they needed to stay out of sight – just in case. He'd slept in worse, much worse! It was miracle enough that it existed – there really was a boat, and a seaworthy one according to Waterman. Soon God willing, they'd sail away, away from the past, away from memories. Would they pursue him still? He supposed they would, they were hard to erase, but perhaps they'd fade.

An odd feeling awoke him as the cabin swayed. Had the boat pulled free? Stumbling in the darkness he groped his way on deck. A figure stood silhouetted against the sunrise – Waterman.

"Sh!" he hissed warningly as Vince edged out onto the deck. "Water high. See she move." Vince nodded, reassured, and returned to his bunk.

Long wait over, tide receded, they set about freeing and shoring up the craft, hacking or dragging away encumbering debris.

"Ok, good. She ready." Waterman grinned expectantly.

"So, what now?"

"We wait! Let water to do work." He slid back up the netting followed by the others.

"How long?" Vince asked, wishing they'd brought more in the way of provisions.

"Before sun come, like night. We go to deep water. There, be big cliff. Water deep, don't see there."

"You've been planning this a long time ..."

"When found her I plan. Lots do before sail. Need water and gas, tank not full."

"Food too!"

"Yes, food. Maybe we find fish, maybe no."

Vince couldn't sleep, his belly was growling. He'd searched the galley, but little consumable was left. He suspected from a few empty cans scattered around, Waterman himself may have eaten it, unless of course some of the crew had survived? It bothered him this lack of bodies.

He woke to Alex shaking his shoulder.

"She's moving!" he gasped. Vince rose instantly, following him up on deck. It was still dark, the sun yet to show its face. Others appeared, alerted by creaks as the ship struggled to right itself.

Vince grabbed at a rope as the deck slid beneath his feet. The vessel rose suddenly in the water. Waterman was jubilant.

"She move! She move!" He ran to take the wheel, steering towards the deep water. "Sail, need sail!" He called urgently. "Vince, take wheel, go to cliff. Need sail." Dashing off, gesturing the others to follow, he began yelling orders. Canvas billowed out, catching the wind. Vince felt the tug on the craft, adjusting the steering. She began to pull away, heading for deeper water. He'd expected a slow shifting, gradually raising them. The sudden tilt had caught them by surprise, even Waterman it seemed. Still, they were safely underway now, the mess of mud and shattered craft falling behind.

Anchored in the shadow of the cliff, Vince watched the first glimmers of sunrise.

"We take little boat, you and me," Waterman gestured. "Tell John. It safe here ... they clean, scrub water tanks ... I tell how, what to use. We go, sun coming." Vince nodded.

3

Stomach growling, Vince fell upon the food, glad he was no longer stranded on the ship.

"So, what happens now?" John asked.

"We need to stock up on food and water. We can lower it down the cliff and take it out on the row boat. Couldn't see a way up, it's pretty sheer, but we have ropes. We could set up a winch of some sort, easier to go that way, closer too."

Waterman set off with a couple of John's guys to help with the cleaning and bring some much-needed provisions aboard. He waved farewell, his usual cowed, fearful, expression turned to hopeful euphoria since the rising of the vessel.

"Seems he's living up to his part of the bargain," John said.

"He's definitely got the skills, should have seen him when we lifted. That current could have taken us right into the swamp or something. He had it under control in minutes, even with a rooky crew – didn't even use the engine. I still think he's hiding stuff though ..."

Vince stood back to watch as the horses returned, loaded with fresh water to be winched down the cliff.

"It's going well," John smiled. "A couple of days should do it.'

"If we can find food that is. How are the savaging teams doing?" The smile faded.

"Not well, gleaning a bit here and there, but nowhere near enough for the trip ... maybe we should just go. Waterman seems to know how to fish ..." Vince glared.

"You can if you want, but I ain't getting on that ship unless we're fully stocked. You heard what he said about the red tide, killed every fish for miles!"

"But ..." Vince raised a restraining hand. John new better than to continue. Vince was an unknown quantity, one he wasn't used to dealing with.

Leaving the men to berth aboard ship, Vince returned to camp with John, Alex and Waterman, bringing the ponies along to shift the rest of their provisions to the cliff top the following morning. They were greeted by an ecstatic waving of hands.

"Food! We found food!" one was yelling. John laughed his relief. Vince sighed, irritated. Still if there was food it solved the problem ...

Bounding into camp John inspected the huge pile of cans Vince followed more slowly, considering. Perhaps John was right, his childlike faith seemed to have triumphed again. He noticed Waterman also did not join the rejoicing. If anything, he was slipping away behind the horses? He broke into a run as Vince spotted him. Dropping the halters, Vince dashed in pursuit. Minus the benefit of cover, he swiftly downed his prey, marching him squirming into camp, his face, white as a sheet, visibly trembling.

"Let go! Please, let go!" he whimpered. "You not understand ... you not know what they do."

"Tell me!" Vince shook him. But he knew already, the empty

boats, the cleared shelves. They must have discovered a storage area for whoever "they" were. Waterman confirmed his worse fears. Staggering into the throng, Vince demanded where they'd found the cans. They pointed.

"Down in the town." Waterman nodded, smiles diminished as they realised something was wrong.

"We need to get out, now! Get the horses loaded up, quickly! Take the food, the rest doesn't matter!"

"But what ...?" John questioned.

"We've just stirred up a hornet's nest! That's what! We need to get going before they wake up to what's happened. How often do they check the supplies?" Waterman shrugged helplessly. "Now listen. Ain't no use you heading off alone. You're safer here with us – with me. I'm going to get us out of here. You understand!" Waterman nodded. "Now, help get everything loaded up."

All seemed well as they huddled along towards the cliff. Tired from their day and loaded down with provisions, the ponies were barely staggering along under their loads.

"Looks like we're gonna make it," John whispered.

"Not there yet. I've a feeling we're being followed. Listen John ... if it comes down to it take Waterman and as many as can make it. Make for the ship. Take the boat out into deep water, the rowboat too so they can't reach you. Listen to Waterman, he knows the tides and the vessel. If he says go, go!"

"But ..."

"No buts, John. If they come, I'll try to hold them off. You get the rest out. You won't be doing me no favours by hanging around, I work better alone."

"We couldn't leave you behind."

"You might have to. The important thing is that you get these guys off safely. I'm pretty good at surviving. Maybe wait awhile before you sail, but don't be drawn back on land. If I make it, I'll swim out. Maybe you could pray for one those messengers to come rescue me again!" Vince chuckled. He was cut short. "Listen!" he hissed, "did you hear that?" John looked blank. "I heard something, up on that ridge. Might be nothing, but best I check it out ... remember what I said!" John nodded as Vince slunk away.

There he was, hunkered down between the rocks. Vince slipped the knife from his belt. They'd said no guns, but this was different ... Soundlessly the knife penetrated lung then heart, no sound issued forth, scarcely knew what hit him. If you had to go that was the way. Taking the automatic, he smiled. This he knew about, kill or be killed, surely the messengers would understand? He checked the area. No sign of anyone else, but that didn't mean they were safe. There'd been no radio, but somehow word had gotten out, that was clear. It worried him they'd gained access to the food so easily. Perhaps it was a set up? Either way he'd best get back to the others ...

John looked up as Vince scrambled back.

"Nothing huh?"

"Oh no, there was someone alright. Had this trained on your heads," Vince showed the automatic. John blanched. "Don't worry, he won't be needing it anymore." John refrained from asking the obvious question. There was a troubling light in Vince's eye.

"Better get a move on. Those who can, go ahead, start winching the stuff down. It's gonna take a few trips to get this all aboard and I'd sooner not do it under gun fire." John gave the order and the line began to expand. "You go too, I'll stay with the ponies and bring up the rear. Take Waterman, make sure he goes on the first trip out, but be sure there's someone to stop him casting off before time. John nodded. Pausing he turned.

"Look," he whispered. "I won't say I haven't had my doubts about taking you from time to time, but you're a good man Vince. If we don't see each other again I'm going to be praying for you night and day, you hear me?" Vince nodded. Wiping a sleeve across his eyes, John called Waterman.

Loaded down and exhausted by their days work the ponies could not be hustled. Pulling two behind him, Vince eyed the surrounding terrain. Alex now pulled the other two, having swapped places at Vince's request. Alex could handle himself if it came to it. The others were well ahead now. He could see silhouettes against the dark blotch of the cliff. Loading had begun.

Automatic bouncing at his hip, brain scrambling tactics, Vince urged the beasts on. Perhaps he could make a trade, exhausted as they were ponies would be valuable. No, they'd not trade, why trade when they could take? They'd want them alive though. A plan formed. Gesturing to Alex he filled him in.

"Poor, bloody blighters," Alex responded. He'd grown fond of the beasts.

"Don't get soft!" Vince hissed. "Can't take them with us anyhow. They've got a better chance of survival than us." It began to rain, adding to their frustrations.

Hope rose as they neared the cliff, the winch and its accompanying silhouettes visible against the sky line. Maybe they'd make it after all ... Gunfire rang out, spinning dust eddies alongside them!

"Go Alex! Go!" Vince yelled, swinging the ponies around, hauling viciously on the reigns as, petrified, they tried to bolt. Alex dragged his two in the direction of the winch, edging them between him and the gun fire, fear picking up the pace.

"Stop right there!" a voice yelled.

"I'm armed!" Vince returned, letting off a few bullets into the air as proof, further frightening the beasts. "I'll trade you the horses if you let us go. I'm special forces, I'd take a good few of you down with me."

"Ain't none of them left! Dead the lot of them! You're bluffing."

"Well I ain't dead, come, try me! Ask yourselves where I got the gun!" There was silence a few minutes. Vince watched Alex heading rapidly for the cliff. A trail of bullets pursued him licking the ground around, but it seemed Vince was correct, they wanted the horses alive. They needed time to offload and winch the stuff down though. Alex was to go ahead, get everyone down, but leave the rope for him – if he made it. While making an effective shield, the horses would pull off his aim.

Damn. Brady would be furious if he messed this up, Dirk thought. What the hell were they doing up here anyway? He'd have made across country if it had been him. His eyes took in movement on the ground above, the same spot the foremost guy seemed to be heading. Nothing there but a cliff face, they'd boxed themselves in ... His attention was drawn by the voice below.

"Well you want them or not?"

"Leave them there and we'll let you go."

"Think I'm dumb or something! Come down where I can see you and get them, or I'll be on my way." The figure edged forward keeping between the ponie's heads. They needed those horses, already two were edging away. Let them, he'd get them later. This guy was the problem, maybe he was who he said he was.

"Fire over the horse's heads," he ordered, "and make damn sure you don't hit one."

The horses reared and twisted but not enough for a clear shot.

"Circle round, get him from behind," he motioned to two of his men. "an' mind those ponies! Brady wants 'em an' I wouldn't like to be in your shoes if you put a bullet in one of them." The men slunk off behind the cover of the ridge.

Vince struggled to hold the ponies, hands gripping tightly close to the bits. Was this a diversion or were they hoping to expose him? One thing was sure, they weren't prepared to risk the ponies.

Alex was almost there. Firing had ceased. Probably trying to outflank me, Vince surmised, that's what he'd do. He pulled the struggling horses bit by bit towards the winch. If he could just get close enough to make a run for it. Not yet though, Alex needed to winch down the saddle bags. The remaining ones were a lost cause. It would be short rations unless Waterman could bag some fish. One thing at a time, get as close as he could ...

What the hell was going on! Dirk thought. The other two ponies were trotting back toward them. It made no sense! Perhaps they'd escaped? They were moving faster than before ... It dawned on him, the cliff top shapes suddenly made sense. They were hauling it down the cliff. They had a vessel waiting!

"Get those horses!" he yelled.

"What about the guy with the automatic?"

"He's not gonna bother you, can't take horses down a cliff. The trade was a diversion, so the others could get away. But he ain't going nowhere. We can say goodbye to half the stuff. Even if we get the ponies there's gonna be hell to pay. We need a scapegoat, and I'm thinking that guy will do nicely. Take him alive!"

Vince was close now. The ponies, free of heavy loads, stumbled past, neighing to their compatriots. Again he sought to keep his beasts moving towards the winch. He sensed movement to his right. Spinning he twirled the horses as a shot rang out. Too late! Blood splattered his hand as one of the ponies let out a shriek, reared, then sank to its knees. Vince dove to the ground, gun at the ready. The reins slipped from his hand. He felt a heavy blow to the head as the second pony plunged and reared. All went black.

Peering over the cliff edge Alex saw it all. They had to go, there was no way to save Vince now. He'd been so close, so very close. Skimming down the rope, he motioned to the waiting boat. Pushing off, he leapt aboard.

"Vince?"

"Didn't made it."

"Is he ... dead?"

"Not as far as I could see. They got around behind him. One fired, hit one of the horses. There were no more shots, don't know what happened but Vince went down. Maybe he was taking cover, but he wasn't moving. There was a guy bending over him, tying him up by looks of it. Wouldn't tie up a dead man ..."

The news was relayed to John aboard ship.

"We can't just leave him!" John responded.

"Nothing we can do. There were a bunch of them, all armed by looks of it. Look! Look up there, see them, on the cliff!"

"But what can we do?"

"What he said to do – cast off, head for deeper water. Waterman, get us out of range."

"But ..." Shots rang out over the water.

"Do it Waterman!" Waterman had no hesitation, nails bitten to the quick in anxious anticipation, he revved the engine heading toward the open sea."

"Stop!" John called. "He said to wait, they can't get us this far out. Give him time, maybe he can escape."

"Twenty-four hours," Alex said. "We can give him that, but no more. We lost a bunch of provisions. We'll have to be on half rations as it is unless Waterman can catch us some fish."

"If it weren't for Vince we'd have lost a lot more, maybe even our lives!"

"So, don't make his sacrifice for nothing, do as he said. He could be dead for all we know."

"OK, twenty-four hours!" John disappeared below praying frantically.

The old porch swing, swung back and forth, John savoured the smell of mum's cooking ... the swing tipped abruptly. Muscles clenching, he awoke. It took a moment to get his head together. He was on the boat, the boat to China ... It was tipping alarmingly. They were underway! Dashing aside the blanket, he rushed on deck. The sun was rising, the boat skirting the far edge of the cliff on its way out to sea.

"Stop! Stop!" he yelled. "We have to wait for Vince."

"It's time." Alex spoke firmly, "Vince didn't make it." Waterman shrugged, turning back to the wheel.

"But we have to do something!"

"Nothing we can do." Alex was having his own battles, but knew well enough they had to go. "He'd hoped John would sleep through their departure.

"There must be something!" John's eyes lit on the little boat bobbing in their wake. "The rowboat, let's at least leave him the row boat. We have a dingy. The current runs that way. If we release it now it would drift ashore like the ship was going to when it lifted."

"OK, OK, if you think it might help." Alex doubted it, stifling his question as to what the hell use it would be. If it made John feel better ...

"At least he'd know we cared ..." John muttered.

4

The children grouped around, some with bunched wildflowers to lay on the grave. Here was a good place for him, overlooking the ocean, far above the city ruins. One of the boys pulled out a homemade bamboo pipe. Notes rang out over the hillside. Not the beauteous sounds Si wan had rendered, but the simple childish notes were somehow suited. He was no longer Si wan the courtesan, no longer a toy of the elite, he was a free spirit now, gone to join the ghosts of his ancestors. Hualien was known for its ghosts, ghosts of the martyrs, of those who left to fight the Supreme leader, the American GI ghosts of WW2, ghosts of Japanese, ghosts of the Dutch, ancient, ancient ghosts. They'd all wanted the island. Now they were all gone, perhaps only she and the children remained.

Sadly, they wandered down toward the paddy fields. She felt a hand pull on her shirt.

"Li Hau, will he ever come back to us?" the eyes looked to her for reassurance. There was none to give.

"He's at rest now, little one. We must let him go. I'm sure he'll be watching over us all."

"Do you think he can be happy without us."

"I'm sure he'll miss you all, but yes, I think he's happy... he was very sick and that made him sad. Perhaps he's looking down on us right now from the clouds." The little head titled upwards.

"It's very beautiful up there. I'm glad he's somewhere nice."

"We'll make it nice again here too, you'll see. One day when the boys are bigger and can help me, we'll build a new village, even better than the old ones. There'll be lots of rice, and fish, bananas and coconuts to spare. See how fast the bamboo grows. One day there will be plenty of everything and only us to eat it all!" The child chucked.

Looking out over the windswept ocean Li Hua felt very alone. She remembered when Si wan had whispered his secret, shown her where he had hidden them away. Since then many had come, so many little mouths to feed, so many hearts to watch over. She'd never had a child of her own, never wanted one. She knew what they'd whispered behind her back, some of the old women. They hadn't refused the food she'd brought though .. Now, now she was mother to so many ...

Head pounding, Vince tested the ropes, his hands and feet looped together under the horse's belly. Whoever tied him knew what they were doing. No way was he gonna get free. He'd been so close, so very close! If not for that confounded pony! Luck of the draw. If he'd remained standing, they'd have shot him anyhow. The question was, why were they keeping him alive? They must want him for something. Whatever it was it wouldn't be pleasant ... He scrutinised the beasts trotting alongside, the man leading them ... Better they thought him unconscious, more possibility of escape. Escape? Who was he trying to fool? These guys knew their trade ...

He picked up words here and there. There was talk of Brady, anger over the dead pony, disturbing chuckles about "a scapegoat", snatches of plans. Brady was obviously the top guy and no prizes as to who the scapegoat might be ... The beasts picked their way dejectedly back toward the town, the other two veering off as they approached. Finally, coming to a stop, he was cut loose and hauled off the pony. Muscles tensed as he slid from its back. The game was up!

"Awake huh!" a blow sent him reeling.

He came to, shrouded in darkness, hands and feet bound tight above and below. Something scurried past his foot, a rat? He tugged at his bindings, no give, again the knots were well tied, immobilising him. There was nothing to be done but ponder what fate they had in store for him. He knew John would wait, but as the hours ticked by, hope dwindled. At least the others would make it, Alex would follow instructions, be sure John didn't do anything stupid. Waterman would be only too keen to cast off. What was it that so terrified him? He had a feeling he was about to find out and, for all his bravado, he was scared.

Voices roused him from his contemplations, laughter – the disturbing kind. His heart raced. Light dazzled his eyes as an oil lamp appeared, preceding two sneering faces.

"You got a visitor coming!" Dirk leered. "Brady's mad about Hank's death, not to mention that pony ... pretty upset about the pony!" They laughed. So that was it, he'd thought as much. He'd have preferred a quick death, but perhaps he deserved to suffer ...

The door opened. A woman appeared, flanked by two body-guards. Tall, leggy, with a mop of long blonde hair, early forties perhaps, but beautiful – Brady's woman probably, come to watch the show. She took her time, looking him over, her voice husky and low with a disquieting edge.

"So, you took out Hank, and one of the ponies."

"I didn't shoot the pony, if they're trying to pin that on me. Your sharp shooters ain't so sharp." She looked questioningly at Dirk. A faint smile tilting her mouth.

"And you're better I suppose?"

"Definitely." A glimmer of hope shimmered. Brady would be a man down. Perhaps this blonde bimbo might put in a word if he played his cards right.

"And you could prove that?" She slid a nail provocatively down his chest to his belt. He gasped, caught off guard as blood rushed to his lions. It had been a long time ... She laughed, enjoying his momentary confusion. "And what else could you prove soldier? They said you were special forces. That true?"

"Yeah, it's true."

"Special forces are all dead! You're lying!" Abruptly a knife was at his throat. This was no kitten.

"I deserted a long time back. Joined the rebels." He kept his voice even, show any weakness and he was dead, probably slowly and painfully dead. Better to go fast if it came to it.

"So, you got special skills huh!"

"If you take that knife away and tell Brady to try me out, I'd be happy to prove it." The face erupted into laughter.

"You men are all alike! Who do you think I am, huh? I am Brady, you fool! Did you think I was some dumb blonde whore? I don't like that, don't like that at all." The knife grazed his chest leaving a welling red smear in its wake. "But at least you're no pussy, that's for sure." Her eyes flashed at Dirk. "I just might let you live. You could be useful ... maybe. What were you doing with those guys? What brings you here?" Vince thought fast.

"They hired me. I was their bodyguard."

"What were they giving you? Money's not much use anymore."

"Food." She nodded acknowledgement. "They had plenty when we set out, but we had to detour 'cos of this crevasse and it started to run out."

"So you decided to steal ours!"

"It wasn't intentional. Those guys are still wet behind the ears. Didn't even know you were here, idiots! Left me to try to sort it out. Mistake taking up with them, no food anywhere else to be had though. Beggars can't be choosers."

"If they were as dumb as you make out, why didn't you just take it?" Vince pondered. Play his card, risk all on this throw? "They said there were women where they were going. Ain't been near a woman in years."

"So I noticed," she chuckled. Was she taking the bait? "We have food, and women, if you're so inclined."

"But Brady, he ..." A look silenced Dirk.

"We need a replacement for Hank. One with brains in his head. But first we need to see if he is what he says he is ... Perhaps we could organise a little sport. Him against you, Dirk, seems fitting. No weapons though, don't want to lose any more men. Here, give me that!" She gestured to Dirk's automatic, levelling it at Vince's face. "Don't think I don't know how to use this soldier, that would be a mistake." Vince didn't doubt her for one minute.

He rubbed his wrists as circulation was restored in painful pins and needles. He made no attempt at escape. With three guns trained on him he'd never make it through the door ...

They emerged in what had once been a basketball court, the poles warped and twisted at either end, a deluge of rubble filling one corner. He noticed Dirk's companion slip him a knife. He'd not expected them to play fair, he knew their sort. A cry went up and others appeared, they had an audience it seemed.

Warily they circled each other, seeking a weakness. Where had he put the knife? Dirk made a grab at him seeking to come to grips. Vince dodged. Better to keep his distance till he knew.

"This is getting boring. Thought you had skills," Brady taunted.

"He has a knife." Vince hissed.

"Sooo ... Let's see you get it off him." Dirk smiled, whipping it from his sleeve. Vince had him in that instant, grabbing the hand and knocking the feet from under him. The knife fell as Vince twisted the arm back, out of its socket. Taken by surprise Dirk yelled but could not escape the grip on his dislocated arm. Cries and yells let out among the crowd. Vince levered him to the ground. Setting one foot to press the wrist into Dirk's back Vince swooped down on the knife, tossing it nonchalantly to Brady.

"Impressive!" she cooed. "Let's see if you can do it again?" She passed it to one of her bodyguards who took up his stance opposite Vince.

With a swift kick to the stomach Vince leapt clear of Dirk. He needed to end this swiftly lest it turned two against one. That would not be easy. His opponent was on guard and probably a skilled fighter or Brady wouldn't have tossed him the knife.

Circling, he took in his adversary – tall, middle-aged, eyes like flint. The knife slashed the air. Vince dodged, anticipating the move, watching, waiting for his chance. Mind racing, he saw his opportunity and took it. Feinting a move to the left, he spun on his heels dashing towards the mound of debris. Calls of derision broke out, but Vince had no mind to run. Grabbing the beam, he swung it to his shoulders flooring his pursuer. Bringing the plank down hard on the wrist he kicked the knife out of reach. It flew across the concrete where it was siezed by one of the onlookers, eager to join the fray.

"Enough!" Brady's voice rang out. "Anyone who can outwit Bruno, deserves a place." It seemed everyone was not of the same opinion. He'd have to watch his back.

"Come, let's talk. I keep the automatic, you get your hands tied, till I decide what to do with you, agreed?"

"You're the boss."

"First show me your hand. The other hand!" Turning it over she felt along the scar. "You dug it out? Why?"

"Told you, I joined the rebels." She nodded, and Vince submitted to a zealous tying of hands, the end of the rope being handed to Brady.

"Bruno, take care of that wrist. Mike, come with me, I may need you." With that she headed off, Vince followed meekly. There was no way he'd make the boat, even if he could get away, which was doubtful. Better to play the henchman till he could figure something out. With John gone there'd be no food, nothing to shoot even if he managed to get a gun, and they'd be watching ...

She led through ruined streets emerging at an old stone building, engulfed with debris, but mostly standing. Inside however was a different story, drapes and elaborate furniture decked the rooms. Whether left by the previous occupants or assembled from various sources, he couldn't tell, but the taste was impeccable.

"Nice place you have here," he ventured. She turned.

"Should have seen my old place. This is nothing by comparison, but hey at least it's standing. They don't have anything like this, don't have the eye for it."

"They?"

"The raiders. Live like rats, always trying to get our food

stores."

"So, there's a rival gang?"

"Gang! Gang!" She heaved abruptly on the rope setting Vince off balance. She was surprisingly strong for a woman. Her henchman levelled a revolver.

"Sorry, sorry!" He raised his hands in supplication.

"Don't you ever use that word again! You hear me!" Vince nodded. Being around Brady was like stepping on thin ice.

They entered what were apparently Brady's private quarters. A dressing table and mahogany bed took up a good deal of the space, a lavish carpet graced the floor. She had an eye for luxury.

"Tie him up." She gestured to the bedpost.

"Don't flatter yourself, that bed's the sturdiest thing around here." Brady interrupted his racing thoughts. "Don't want you breaking free, such a waste ..." She brandished the automatic, waving dismissively for Mike to leave.

"He'll be right outside. Now, tell me about yourself. First your name."

"Vince," may as well use his real name, no records anyway.

"And ... what made you leave the force?"

"They killed my kid brother. I wanted to get even."

"And did you?"

"Not with that guy, but I got plenty more." She laughed.

"Revenge is a sweet dish huh? One of my favourites."

"It helps. So, what did they do to you?"

"Sure you could guess ..." He had to watch his words. Play the safe bet.

"They hurt someone you cared about?"

"Pansy!" She prodded the automatic under his chin. "No, they hurt me. Coming here, taking over ..." It dawned on Vince.

"You were a show girl."

"Damn right I was, one of the best!"

"I can see that." Vince didn't do flattery, but the gun was unnerving ... it wasn't flattery anyway, she still had that charisma about her.

"Turned us into whores, common whores. But I found me a

38

man with connections, and I got my revenge. I saw that bastard grovel and beg at my knees."

"You killed him?"

"Killed him, no. That would be too easy. I found a far more appropriate method of revenge." She gestured to a glass jar on the dressing table. Vince blanched at the contents. "Died anyway it turns out, bled to death before they found him. Now I'm the boss."

"What about the guy who helped you?"

"Dead. Died along with everyone else who got those implants."

"They all died?"

"You didn't know?"

"I only knew the government forces were wiped out somehow. But, was it the chips?"

"Sure was, some kind of electronic pulse, one minute here, the next gone."

"Civilians too?"

"Every last one of them including some of my girls."

"How come you didn't ..."

"They didn't want records, kept us tucked away in secret, for officers use only. After I escaped and hooked up with Al. I sure as hell wasn't gonna have anything to do with government. I made a deal. Los Vegas showgirls fetch a good price and my girls were well looked after. They didn't mind a sugar daddy or two as long as they had a say."

"What about the military? Didn't they ...?"

"They were our biggest customers. Word got around what happened to the general, after that most preferred to deal through Al. Didn't know he was involved, the fools ... How come you don't know about all this stuff? Been off in the backwoods?"

"Pretty much. Wyoming, nothing but trees and critters."

"Not much of rebels then."

"Not enough of us to take them on in the cities, but out there, on our territory, we could knock them off a few at a time. I wasn't looking to bring down the regime, just looking out for number one and getting some vengeance at the same time." The words sounded false as they rolled off his tongue. They'd always been false he realised. Even in the early days it had been his commitment to Chad that kept him. Without it, would he have turned out like Brady? Was he like her even now?

"So, I must decide what to do with you. You seem a bit of a kindred spirit. You got skills we need, plus, you're in pretty good shape, good genes and all."

"What?"

"Oh come on, most of the population's dead, gotta think ahead, choose the best stock."

"Like a prize bull?"

"Something like that," she slid him a scorching glance.

"Look, I'm pretty attached to my balls lady ..."

"Not with me, idiot. I told you, we got women here. I could hook you up with one of my girls – no more paying customers around. But I've a mind to see if you're up to the job first ..." She slid the gun provocatively up his thigh.

"I'm more than up for it."

"So I see!" She laughed, enjoying the torment she was causing him. Vince was thinking fast, trying unsuccessfully to ignore the pulsing throb in his loins. This woman was dangerous. "You may as well resign yourself to staying here," she continued. "No food for miles around, and winter will come, even if you managed to get free without getting shot, you'd die of starvation."

"What is it you want exactly? I'm good with a gun, and I got tactical stuff to offer. As long as there's food I'll do whatever, and if you want to use me as your prize bull, I've no objection, quite the reverse."

"Not my prize bull, one of several. You fought one today."

"Bruno?"

"Yeah, Bruno. He does the rounds."

"When can I start?"

She laughed, calling the guard. "Put him with Candy. Set a guard on the door though."

"I'll have them send food up. Tomorrow you take over Bruno's job till his wrist's healed," she added as she strode out.

5

"So, guess you're Brady's new prodigy." Glazed eyes assessed him as the guard untied the rope and edged out of Candy's door. "So, guess that makes me expendable, huh!"

"No way I'm gonna hurt you lady. I'd prefer not to add my balls to Brady's collection"

She laughed. "Smart guy huh! Well all the better for me Drink? Only got scotch, you OK with that."

"Scotch would be great!" She was already half gilded. He appraised her as she poured the drinks. She'd be pretty if not in such a mess. Auburn curls cascaded down her back contrasting with a stained dressing gown, through which he traced her curves.

"Not too much for you," she giggled. "You gotta perform and all."

"A glass or two of scotch isn't gonna impede that any. It's been a long time ..."

"Yeah? Brady likes results! Not that it'll do you much good, not with me."

"Why?" What was he missing here?

"Don't work with me ... unfertile ..." she slurred the word derisively. "Don't think she'd put you in with one the good breeders, do you? Me, I'm expendable ..."

"In that case we'll just have us some fun." He took the glass from her hand. "Think you've had enough for now."

"Ain't never had enough." She reached for the glass, but he pushed it further away.

"I like a woman who can't get enough." He silenced her response with a kiss, slipping his hand under the satin robe. God, he was hard as nails ...

Breathless, he lay satiated on the bed.

"I'd forgotten how good it was!" he panted. She laughed, leaning to grab the glass. He caught her arm. "You're one beautiful lady, you know that?"

"Don't count for nothing these days, if you can't breed."

"Counts for me. Lay off that stuff a while huh! There's better things to do."

"Like what?" He slid his hand possessively over her thigh. She smiled, slow and sultry. "You up for that?"

"You bet I am."

A niose at the door interrupted them. The guard entered carrying a tray of food.

"You don't waste no time, do you?" He leered.

"Be off with you Tom, got my hands full," she sneered.

"Can see that." Seizing the glass, she hurled it at the closing door, scattering whiskey dregs and shards of shattered glass.

"Damn old goat!"

"Don't seem to like him much."

"No reason to, hangs around here, sniffing for what he might get."

"Thought Brady made sure her guys' needs were met?"

"Only her favourites, the rest fend for themselves. Ain't so bad, she has taste, I'll say that for her." She slid a hand appreciatively over his chest."

"So, you getting a taste for me Candy?"

"Maybe, try again and see." The hand moved down, Vince gasped.

The door flew open rousing them from sleep.

"Hell, don't you ever knock?!" Candy yelled, throwing a sheet over her. Tom grinned, motioning to Vince.

"Fun's over. Bruno's on his way, get some clothes on." Vince swore, grabbing at his boxers. He bent over Candy's rumpled hair as he made for the door.

"Lay off the bottle and I promise you some fun if I make it back," he whispered. Candy groaned, her head pulsating. Bruno was waiting, arm bound across his chest.

"Don't get any ideas," he hissed. "Brady's apt to change her mind, and when she does, we have a score to settle." He waved the automatic balanced in his good arm. Vince said nothing.

"Sooo ... been busy have we?" Brady purred as Vince was passed on to Mike, Brady's remaining bodyguard.

"You could say that." She glided across the floor towards them, robe gaping slightly at the neck. Even a night with Candy barely took the edge off. She clearly enjoyed her power. Vince averted his gaze from her cleavage.

"Time to get down to work ..." She slid her nail over the swell of his arm in that way she had. "You take Bruno's place which means you stay a step behind and on the watch. No gun just yet."

With infinite relief Vince slid into Candy's room, nerves frayed, brain frazzled from the day's endless tightrope walk with Brady. He had to get out of here!

Candy was drunk again. Walking to the bottle, he poured himself a stiff one.

"Where'd you get this stuff anyway?"

"We got plenty left from the old days. The guys bring me a bottle or two from time to time." I bet they do, Vince thought, he could figure the rate of exchange – none of his business ...

"I could use one myself!" He gulped it back and poured another.

"Tough day?"

"Yeah."

"You need a little fun?" She slid her hands seductively around his neck.

"Maybe. Thought I asked you to stay off the bottle though?"

"You don't own me!" Green eyes flashed.

"Never said I did, but I'd prefer you weren't so gilded." Sliding his hands down over her buttocks, he pulled her against him. She laughed.

"Don't seem to put you off much." She pulled his head down to hers, then let her fingers explore hungrily. All thought of escape faded ...

She was more vocal this time, crying out as he finished, matching his timing to her own. Intense frustration appeased, old skills were returning. Rolling aside, he stopped her arm groping for the glass.

"What is it with you? Don't even want a girl to have a drink? The others don't mind!"

"Look lady," he pinned her hands beside her head, looking down at her. "It's gonna kill you that stuff. First it'll take your looks ..."

"What do you care?"

"Like I said, you're a pretty lady. I like my women that way. Don't waste it, at least not when you're with me. I like your full attention. Hurts a guy's pride when a woman has to get gilded before she'll go with him." She laughed.

"That's not why I drink. Not with you anyway."

"Maybe, maybe not, it'd be nice just once to make out when you were sober, so I'd know. What's with the drinking anyway?"

A sulky, childlike, pout distorted her features, "I had top guys wrapped around my finger, buying me stuff and pampering me. Now, now, like I said, I'm expendable. Brady keeps me for the dregs. Beauty's no use anymore. They're dead those guys, all dead! Now it only matters if you conceive ..." Tears flooded her eyes. Vince pulled her to his shoulder. He'd been so long away from a woman he'd forgotten how soft and fragile they could be sometimes. God knows, Anne, the only woman among the vigilantes, had been anything but soft! Candy clung sobbing, and somehow, after a day of Brady's high-handed treatment, it felt good.

Morning came, again the door was thrust open, again he was escorted to Brady, and this time given a gun. He pondered.

"Trouble with raiders, you might need it, "she said by way of explanation, striding off. Glancing at Mike, he followed, taking up his usual rear-guard position.

He hadn't visited this part of the city. He scanned the area. Perfect place for an ambush, half ruined buildings, plenty of cover. Something was wrong, just what he couldn't say. He fingered the automatic. Should he make a break for it? No way, this had all the ingredients of a set up ...

Shots rang out. Diving to the floor, he pulled Brady down with him. Mike likewise hit the deck. He gestured to an overturned car.

"Better cover over there, keep down! There's a sniper up there in that window." Mike hung back, covering them, as he and Brady crawled behind the wrecked vehicle. "Stay here! I'll go see if I can flush him out." Brady nodded. He fired a couple of rounds then made a dash for cover closer to the place the shots came from. Mike had joined Brady behind the car, it looked like he was coming after him. Whatever Brady's motivation in giving him the gun, he didn't trust Mike one iota. Should he run for it?

Slamming into the doorway he mounted the stairs, gun at the ready. Shots rang out from the upstairs room. Edging past the piled debris of the upper story he took a deep breath. A well-aimed kick decimated the crumbling door. Bursting in, he let go a volley of gunfire. A figure, crouched by the window, fell under the impact. Footsteps sounded on the stairs behind him. He turned, expecting Mike. Instead Brady stood there, hands on hips. The figure at the window regained his feet. No blood! They'd given him blanks, set him up to see what he'd do. Good he hadn't made a run for it.

"You set me up!"

"Sure we did. Didn't think I'd go giving you live ammo." Vince played dumb. "Do you really think I'd need a man to rid me of one pesky sniper?" Brady continued.

"Why the bodyguards then?"

"Just in case anyone gets ideas about who runs this family. You did good, moved up a grade ... Still on probation though." If Brady was pleased, Mike was not. Evidently he'd been hoping to put a bullet in Vince's back. He'd killed one of their own, not only that, he was competition. He kept to himself as they trudged back to the main house.

That night he was invited to eat with the others. The food was significantly better, a kind of meat stew, tough, but a definite improvement on the canned hash he'd been served previously. He looked around the tables, must be about twenty guys in all – a lot of mouths to feed. Then there were the women, two sporting enlarged bellies, one with a babe in arms. They weren't as pretty as Candy, at least he didn't think so. They seemed to have let themselves go, or perhaps they were smart enough not to compete with Brady ...

He ate in silence ignoring the glaring looks of the woman with the child. Finishing quickly, he headed off toward Candy's room.

"Where are you going?" Brady glanced a proprietary eye in his direction.

"Thought I'd turn in for the night."

"We're not finished here. Leastways I'm not finished." Vince resumed his seat. "We like to have a bit of fun of an evening sometimes, keeps the guys in shape." Alarm bells rang. What was she up to?

"Now see, I've demoted Dirk, since the cliff top fiasco, 'sides Mona there already has one of his." She nodded at the baby. "Good to diversify don't you think?"

"I thought you wanted to pair me up with Candy? I got a thing for redheads," Vince tried his hand, this looked like trouble.

"Huh! You men are all the same! Candy's sterile, everyone knows it. If you're a good boy and do your duty by Mona, maybe I'll let you sidle up with Candy now and then. 'Course first you gotta fight for it, other guys are not as picky as you. Just wrestling, don't want to damage the goods, do we?" She laughed. It was as Vince feared. Would he have to take on a bunch together, for sure they'd go for him before fighting among themselves.

"So, do we have contenders?" Mike stood. "Not you Mike. You already got a kid and a woman, what do you need another for?"

"I don't, just want to ram his teeth down his throat."

"Sit down Mike." Vince took off his shirt in preparation. Brady slid an appreciative eye. Two guys stood, another wavered. It seemed word had spread about his skills. No one wanted to lose face.

"What's the rules?" Vince asked.

"There are none, except you have to hold your opponent on the floor for a count of ten and these guys might count slow.' Brady laughed, waving one of the guys forward. No rules? Suited him.

His first opponent was swiftly eliminated. The second, a giant of a man, stood watching intently.

"So, Sully, now's your chance, we don't have no black babies yet!" Brady quipped. Sully slid off his shirt revealing sleek ebony muscle. "He's had a thing for Mona since the beginning." Brady informed with a smirk. For all Vince cared he was welcome to her, but he couldn't afford to lose face, if you live in a dog pack, safest to be top dog.

Sully moved in fast swinging a massive fist, going for a knock-out punch. Vince dodged, appraising his opponent. He was fast for his size. He swung again. A mistake, Vince caught the punch using the momentum to pull him off balance. For a moment Vince had the upper hand, but a quick roll swept Sully clear and he regained his feet. He was not foolish enough to try that again. Instead he closed with Vince, going for an arm lock and failing as they strove back and forth. Jeers and yells went out as they struggled, well matched in strength and ferocity, doubtless they made a good show.

Vince again caught Sully off balance. As they crashed to the floor, a glint of silver caught his eye, a knife flew across the floor towards Sully's outstretched hand. To Vince's surprise Sully shoved it away.

"I don't need no help to claim what's mine!" he yelled. The distraction proved his downfall as Vince inflicted a well-aimed punch to the abdomen leaving him winded. Seizing the moment, Vince moved into a headlock that drove the winded Sully to the floor. The count began, not as slow as he'd expected. Sully was no more popular than he, particularly since he'd refused the knife. Someone wanted him dead, probably a bunch of them. He thought fast. On the count of nine he released Sully, still winded but able to struggle into a sitting position.

"I only got him because he wouldn't use the knife," Vince announced. "'Sides if things are as bad as you say we'll need some black kids."

"Oh playing the gentleman are we Vince? That's something I'd not expected. Seems you have a bit of a thing for Candy after all."

Sully rose to his feet. "Look, I don't need no favours!" he spat.

"Didn't seem that way to me," Brady announced. "You fought well though Sully, no one's been able to touch this guy and you gave him a run for his money, might even have won had you not been distracted. Maybe I've been overlooking you. None the less, Vince came out on top. So, tell you what I'll do, let's continue the competition, alternate nights, see who gets a baby. For sure we'll know the difference!" She laughed but there was no humour in it. "Your turn tonight Vince and I expect to see results! I may think up a penalty for the loser."

Exactly what had he gotten himself into Vince wondered, pictures of the fateful jar invading his consciousness. Maybe he should have just gone along with it, but somewhere in the back of his mind he'd been relieved when he found Candy couldn't conceive. Could he leave a child to be raised by the likes of Brady?

Mona glowered at him, angry at his rejection. This was not going to be a pleasant night ...

Vince was right, Mona was as responsive as an ice statue. Sullenly she slid her dress to the floor and lay glaring at him. He hesitated. Two days ago there would have been no question, but frustration satiated with Candy, he found himself unaroused. Rape had never been his forte, besides there was the jar to worry about damned if he did, damned if he didn't.

"Not good enough for you! Huh? Wish Sully had taken that damn knife and used it!" she hissed.

"You want Sully?"

"Hell, I don't want any of you, but at least he was man enough to fight!" She glared. Vince's mind was working hundred to a dozen. Whatever he said would doubtless reach Brady's ears.

"Look, a man's got pride. I could see you didn't want me. I sure as hell don't want to be forcing my attentions on someone when ..."

"When Candy is only too willing, huh?" He nodded. "She always was a slut!" she hissed. Vince bit back his reply. Mona was, it seemed, an unwilling surrogate mother, but he'd have to watch his step.

"Now I've got two of you, as if Dirk wasn't bad enough!"

"Look, I won't force you."

"And have Brady hear. You have no idea what might happen to me."

"She won't hear it from me, if she don't hear it from you." The eyes faltered.

"You trying to trick me?"

"Nope. I like to get it on as much as the next, but it ain't no fun with an ice queen ..." She had to think it was her idea so she'd keep quiet about it. "Course if you change your mind?" He slid a finger suggestively down her thigh. She jerked away. Had Dirk been rough with her?

"If you say nothing, I won't." The angry glare gone, desperation tinged her gaze. "But what about Sully?"

"You're on your own with that one. But hey, he seems pretty stuck on you from what Brady said. Maybe you two might get it together. You could use a protector around here. Not all men are like Dirk you know ..."

"What do you know about anything?!" Vince backed off, mustn't push his luck.

"So, we got a deal? Candy gives me more than I can handle anyhow. Why should I force you? Not for the moment at least ..." He left her hanging.

"OK ..." Vince heaved a sigh of relief. Come spring he'd find a way to escape long before any child was born.

Slipping off his shirt and pants he lay down, being careful to keep a good distance between them ...

Sully glared as Vince passed in Brady's wake. He'd hoped by his gesture the previous evening he might gain a comrade, instead it seemed he'd only served to infuriate him. Once he'd have expected the animosity, but now ... something had changed. He detested the role he was forced to play. How petty and juvenile the swagger and threats compared to Chad and the other guys. He thought of them often. He even thought of John, his concern and quiet courage. Despite their varied years, these guys were kids by comparison, adolescents with guns and knives ... and Brady, with her mix of sex and fear manipulated them all. He had questions, so many questions he dare not ask.

The day passed without incident. The mysterious "raiders" made no appearance. Brady passed her day organising work crews clearing debris from any semihabitable buildings and adding to winter stores of firewood, together with placing look-outs for the precious food stores. For the moment Vince was exempt from such duties, which, he wondered, would they place him on when Mike's wrist recovered. He'd feel safer behind a gun.

Sully was full of himself that evening, pulling Mona onto his lap and promising, "a night to remember". Vince kept to himself, trying to avoid any further conflicts. With Sully taking centre stage, he found it easy to slip off.

Candy was considerably less gilded he noticed. The auburn curls had been brushed and the robe looked like it had been washed.

"Sooo, you came ... was hoping you would. Wasn't sure you'd get past Brady ... or if you'd want to ..." The eyes looked up questioningly.

"'Course I want to." Vince slipped an arm around her waist. It felt good to feel her, soft and yielding, against him ... She pulled away, tipping her face towards him.

"You didn't come last night. I got drunk, blotto ... Did you like her better than me?" No way was he going to risk telling her his arrangement with Mona.

"What, 'the ice queen'? A man has to do, what a man has to do,

50

but it was like making out with a statue. She ain't nothing compared to you. Anyhow ... told you, I like my ladies pretty. I like redheads too." He wound a curl around his finger.

"I heard about that. Tom told me."

"Yeah, I gotta go with Mona every other night ... but as long as I can ... I'll come back ... here ..." He interspersed the words with kisses working across her jaw and down toward her cleavage. She responded eagerly.

Sated, he lay back on the pillow.

"You want a drink?" She queried.

"I got me all I want right here ... but hey, you been laying off the bottle on my account?"

"Maybe ..." She rolled her eyes provocatively.

"So ... you do have a taste for me then, even when you're sober?"

"Maybe...?" She slid her hand down his side curving round to his groin. "What do you think?"

"I think you need to give a guy a fighting chance," he chuckled. "I ain't recovered from the last session yet." He imprisoned her hands either side of her face, swinging over to cover her. He kept the kisses gentle, he had questions to ask and with Brady around he never knew when he'd next have opportunity. He gently unclenched her hand. He'd been right, no scar. She laughed.

"No, I ain't got one. They kept us secret, off the grid you might say."

"Yeah, Brady told me. But I've noticed some of the guys have them."

"They all have them." She slid the escaped hand enticingly down his buttocks. It was hard to keep this casual. He recaptured it kissing the knuckles.

"How come they ain't dead then?"

"You're full of questions tonight."

"Gotta stay distracted somehow or you'll wear me out." She chuckled, enjoying her power.

"Brady's man had 'friends in high places', contacts and stuff. It didn't do for his henchmen's movements to be tracked, so he bribed one of the guys. They stuck dud implants in. Just the sheath, don't show on any monitor. Now Al, he was the face of the business, he got the real deal. Killed him, along with all the others."

"So Brady took over?"

"Not exactly, some of the guys didn't like the idea of a woman boss. Who do you think the raiders are? Al didn't leave no directions, and he died in her arms you might say, in her bed at least, so she got the jump on the others."

"She got the food."

"Smart boy! Now enough with the diversions. Maybe you ain't ready to go again, but a girl could use a little fun while she's waiting."

"You were right when you said you couldn't get enough."

"Well if you want me to lay off the liquor you gotta keep me distracted other ways."

"You got yourself a deal lady." He didn't want to push too much, he'd found out quite a bit. Besides distracting Candy was something he enjoyed. It made this place liveable.

"Didn't see you last night?" Brady greeted.

"I'd had enough of Sully's boasting. You know what they say about guys like that ..."

"So, strong, silent type, are we?"

"Let's just say if you have the goods you don't need to brag about it."

"And you figure you have, huh!"

"Let's just say I don't need to prove nothing." Thankfully Brady accepted Vince's distain for his opponent as reason to slip off. Tonight was his turn with Mona again. He hoped Sully had done nothing to disturb his plans.

He glimpsed Candy at one point, engaged in scrubbing laundry with one of the other women. It was the first time he'd seen her in anything but the robe, the first he'd seen her out of the room in fact. She looked up and threw a furtive smile. He raised his fingers in acknowledgement. They both knew better than to draw Brady's attention.

"Want to slip off early?" he asked Mona. "We could take our bowls." She nodded. Brady was distracted talking to Bruno, who seemed to feel his wrist sufficiently better to resume his duties and Vince had no wish to be around when Sully came to the table.

"Didn't see you around today?" he said between bites, hoping for more information.

"I work in the kitchen mostly, when I'm not with the baby."

"So, do you like it, cooking I mean?"

"I hate it!" Tears appeared, welling up. He opened his mouth, but she cut him off, anger kindling. "I don't want to talk about it, OK! Look I said we'd come eat, not settle down for a cosy chat. Just because you ain't fucking me doesn't mean you're my friend OK?"

"OK, I just thought ..."

"Well just stop thinking, OK?"

"OK." It seemed the kitchen was a taboo subject as far as Mona was concerned. He'd try another tack later. They continued to eat in silence while Mona calmed down.

"You still OK with our arrangement. You're not going to tell Brady, are you?" There was a quiver to her voice.

"Look, Candy wore me out last night, all I want is a good night's sleep."

"You got a thing for Candy?"

"The sex is good, but I ain't the kind to settle with one woman." He had to play this right. "Course if you've come around?" He grabbed her hand and pulled her towards him. As he'd thought, she pulled away, but not before he saw the bruises on her arm. He looked up questioningly.

"Sully?" She nodded.

"I should have known better. I never could fake it like Candy."

"I'm sorry. I hoped he'd be OK, seeing as how he likes you."

"Well if he does, he has a damned funny way of showing it."

"He's young. How old do you think? Mid-twenties? He sure doesn't look like the type to grow up learning how to treat a woman."

"You can say that again. He wasn't part of the mob ... grew up on the streets mostly – that's where he learnt to fight. He came practically begging for food, Brady took him on, thought he might be useful."

"She was right, fights better than the other guys that's for sure."

"They don't like him 'cause he's black, that and because he wasn't part of the clan, most of these guys are. They don't like you much either."

"Tell me about it! I'm worried if I get put on clearing I might wind up with a knife in my back."

"You're right about that, I'd keep a lookout if I were you."

"Look, about Sully, maybe you could talk to him, try and make him understand. I suspect all this bravado is just a front." She eyed him suspiciously.

"Why you saying all this?"

"I don't like to see pretty ladies getting beat up. Spoils it for the rest of us if one goes too far. Ain't many women left you know ..."

"So, you're like Brady, see us as a commodity to be exploited!" Vince said nothing, better she hated him then he wouldn't have to bed her.

6

Next morning he was roused by Tom. "Come on, no more lazing around with Brady for you. Gonna have to put in a day's work for a change." Vince grabbed his clothes, glad he'd doffed them for appearance sake. Tom was sure to be eyes and ears. Pulling on the T shirt he headed after him.

"You're on Louie's team," Tom tossed over his shoulder, approaching a group of three men, the foremost of which turned with a scowl.

"You're late!" he growled. There was no stop for food, the others having already eaten. Louie deliberately set Vince to clear the heavy stuff. His stomach growled, but he ignored the jibes. At least it seemed they weren't gonna try anything, perhaps his growing rep. put them off, or maybe because of Brady, maybe both. By mid-day he was ravenous. To his surprise Mona appeared with another woman, doling out what looked like a sardine and bean hash. There was no eye contact, but he noticed she gave him a good helping for which he was grateful.

"Not gonna slip off for a quickie then?" Louie jibed. There was resentment smouldering, he could feel it.

"Ain't got the energy! You been working me like a horse." There were mutterings about newcomers and Hank. He ate in silence. The afternoon passed similarly. He kept an eye for potential "accidents" but nothing happened. Maybe Brady had given them a talk.

He came to the table exhausted. Brady and co. were already there, as was Sully, once more full of himself. Vince ignored him, tucking into his stew with relish. He reached for a second bowl. Brady noticed.

"Building up an appetite huh?"

"I missed breakfast."

"Oh, and here I thought you'd been working too hard last night. Eager to get the job done huh?"

He smiled. "I aim to please."

"I can see that. It's been a while since Candy was sober enough to do some work about the place."

"Nothing to do with me."

"Maybe, maybe not. Is he that good in bed Mona?" Mona flushed with anger.

"Candy's a slut. Always has been! Just found someone to keep up with her." Vince breathed a sigh of relief.

"Why here she is now, the lady herself." He drew breath again as Candy joined the table. Not a good idea ...

"So Candy, tell us, what got you off the bottle huh? Something to do with Vince?" Candy looked up flustered.

"I realised when you sent him, I was expendable. He could have killed me! Thought I'd better pull my weight, or I might not be so lucky next time." Candy went up several points in Vince's estimation.

"So Vince ..." Brady swung to face him, "tell me, which is the best fuck, huh?" He thought fast.

"Don't think anyone could beat Candy on that score, but she can't have kids." He saw Candy tear up. He continued, drawing the attention. "I like a bit off diversity though." He slid an eye over Mona infuriating Sully. When he looked up Candy had gone.

"Well you ain't getting no diversity tonight!" Sully slung out. Taking Mona's hand, he pulled her away from the table.

"Sully, wait! I have to nurse the baby."

"Take him with us then!" He swung off abruptly pulling her after him.

Vince rose from his seat, hoping to take advantage of the distraction. No such luck.

"You sneaking off again, Vince?"

"Louie's been working me pretty hard, and like you said, I was up quite a bit last night. A man has to sleep sometimes."

"And where do you sleep Vince? In Candy's room?"

"Ain't been given no other place."

"We'll see about that. You can doss down with the other guys tonight. Tom, show him where." Vince was annoyed. He'd not sleep sound with these guys around, besides he'd looked forward to a night with Candy ...

The old nightmare repeated itself. He was there on the stairway again, waiting ... But there was no Jase, no pattering feet, instead, flames licked towards him. Smoke billowed from above, choking him. He awoke in a cold sweat. It was no dream! Fire was springing across the room catching on the mattresses, licking at the curtains. He ran for the door. It was locked.

Frantically he looked around. The window was boarded, the curtains aflame, but hardboard would yield easier than the door, besides they might have set stuff behind it. He had seconds to decide. Grabbing down the flaming curtains he took a run at the window, kicking hard. It buckled but didn't give way, must be a frame behind it. One more try, more to the left. His clothes were kindling as he smashed his way through, rolling on the ground to extinguish them.

Pain seared his hands and arm, but he was clear. Flames billowed, sucking oxygen through the hole. Better get away, no telling what those guys might do. He could hear them making a racket around by the entrance. His leg hurt from the impact. He was limping, dazed, but combat training kicked in. The fire would wake everyone, wake Brady. There would be hell to pay for this. Doubtless they'd blame him. Best he stay out of sight till the confrontation, somewhere he could hear but not be seen? He strove for focus. No, too risky, they might see the window and come looking. He needed witnesses, only one came to mind He stumbled toward the main house. Already things were stirring.

He pounded on the shutters, the noise hidden by the tumult behind him. God, let her hear, let her be sober enough to hear ...

"Who ... who is it? What do you want?"

"It's me, Vince. Quick, open up!" Shutters opened and there she was, a dishevelled, red eyed, angel. Vince held a scorched finger to his lips, clambering into the bedroom.

"Vince, you're hurt!"

"Sh! Sh! I'm OK. They tried to kill me, but I'm OK. I just need a place to hide till Brady gets there." Candy's eyes grew wide in horror.

"Your hands, your poor hands!"

"Water, I need water, clean and cold." He looked around. The bucket stood in its normal place and he plunged his hands and arm within. "It's a bit late, but it'll be OK. Just surface burns, it'll heal." Candy was biting her knuckles, in an agony of anxiety. "It's OK I tell you. It'll be fine, just keep it quiet OK?" The pain eased a little as the cooling water took effect.

"Candy listen, can you do something for me?" She nodded. "I want you to go down by the doss house. Don't say anything, just tell me what's said, OK. An' don't tell anyone I'm here. If they find out, I'll say you left the door open and I came in after you'd gone."

"OK Vince. I got it." She was taking deep breaths, endeavouring to get under control.

"Look, you're smart Candy. I could see that the way you answered Brady tonight. Though why you came I don't know."

"She made me ... Vince ... what you said about liking diversion, was that true?" The eyes had that hurt look about them. Women! Vince thought exasperated, here I am, barely escaped with my life and she wants to know if I like Mona. Patience, he needed her help.

"Course not Candy. I just don't want Brady thinking there's something going on between us."

"That's what I thought."

"Look you'd better go see what's going on, OK? They'll have cooked up some story to cover their tracks and I need to know what it is."

"OK Vince, I'll go, an' I'll be careful." She brushed his lips in passing as she headed out of the door. He heard her emerge, sounding a good deal more gilded than she was, and adding considerably to the chaos outside. It seemed Brady was not the only one with star abilities. He wondered if the drunkenness might be a front also, he thought not, she'd seemed pretty gilded that first night? Thinking of which he glanced around for Candy's bottle. He could use a stiff drink himself.

She was not long in returning, slipping in quietly, grasping what looked like a sheet in one hand.

"I got this from the laundry. It's clean. Figured you'd need something to cover those burns."

"You never cease to surprise me Candy. So, what's the story?"

"They said it was you of course, that you insisted on having a candle, didn't trust them in the dark. Said they tried to get you out, but you were sleeping too deep and it went up too fast."

"Liars! Did they say anything about the window?"

"Window? No. The whole place went up. Is that how you got out?" Vince nodded.

"Brady there now?"

"Yes and boiling mad. She suspects."

"And they told you I was dead right."

"Yeah."

"OK, we go back together so they don't try and get me on the way. You say ..."

"That I found you stumbling around on my way back."

"Smart girl Candy!"

"You have to be to survive around here."

"OK, let's do it."

As soon as they neared the group, Candy began to pretend to prop him up and call in a wild drunken manner.

"He's here! He's not dead!" Eyes turned, plenty of witnesses Brady strode towards them like a thunderstorm, her usual sarcastic veneer slipped to reveal boiling fury.

"What the hell is going on?"

Vince took a leaf from Candy's book. "I escaped ... through the window ..." he gasped. Better he seemed worse than he was.

"And the candle? Did you have a candle? Mighty funny you escaped through the window if the fire started at your bed!" Her eyes roved accusingly over his opponents.

"Candle? Didn't have no candle ... didn't know we had any ..."

"That's true, how would you know? Maybe we need to do some good old-fashioned investigating once the fire's died down. See if there's any piles of melted wax by his bed. Huh?"

"Couldn't find anything after a fire like that," Louie interposed

"That is where you're wrong Louie. I want answers and I want them fast or I might just decide to start some intensive questioning."

"Look ... I'm OK ... no real harm done ..." Vince wanted leverage with these guys.

"No harm! Look at you, you'll be weeks before you're fit for duties. And what about the hall, where you guys gonna sleep tonight!"

"There's the ..." Louie began.

"There's the nothing! You sleep outside till I get the truth! You understand! As for you Vince. You'd better stay with Candy. Seems you're not safe to sleep elsewhere. And I don't want anymore accidents! That understood! There'll be consequences, you better believe it!" The crowd dispersed rapidly, no one keen to become the target of Brady's wrath. Vince limped back, supported by a wobbling Candy.

Once they regained the room she dissolved into giggles.

"Haven't had that much fun in a while. Feels good to put one over on those guys."

"Glad you enjoyed it, but it's not all put on. Think you could help me bandage my hands up?" Candy sobered.

"Sorry Vince. Course I will. Then I suggest we both have a little nightcap and get some sleep."

"OK, but just the one huh?" She smiled sweetly as she began to tear the sheet into strips.

"Can't believe I have you all to myself for a while."

"Now don't get any ideas Candy? I'm not up for it."

"Not tonight maybe, but tomorrow maybe we can work something out to take your mind off the pain."

Days passed. His hands healed rapidly, but he affected a pronounced limp, enabling him to stay put in the room. Candy continued her laundry duties during the day and Mona brought food. Nothing was said about his resuming his duties in that area. Sully was taking full advantage of the situation it seemed. Candy brought him books to pass the time. There was lots of stuff around she said, you just needed to rifle through the rubble. He wondered if there might be useful stuff. Guns and food supplies were sure to have been scavenged, but perhaps there were maps or tools, even a good kitchen knife would be a help ...

Nights began to resume their former passion, Candy taking a more dominant role due to his injuries. He pumped her for information gaining insight into the inner workings of the group. Organised crime had a long history in Vegas, it seemed, adapting to change as it came, including the recent world government regime. Men would always be men, and Brady, with her show girl credentials had been the perfect foil. She stuck with Al but needed someone for the top brass of the military and local government. Candy had been that someone. Then, every-thing had changed on that fateful day. In an hour it was all gone, nothing but bodies everywhere, dead, all dead!

7

The scent of spring was in the air. He'd planned to go in spring, but life had become easy. Settled back in his old mould, Vince enjoyed a privileged place. He never discovered what happened about the fire, only that upon his summons from Candy's room he found himself elevated to guarding the food supplies. He'd later finally been relegated a gun, having proved his worth and supposed loyalty in a skirmish with the raiders.

Mona had become pregnant in his absence. Sully claimed full ownership and Vince was relieved to have it so. Brady seemed content to trade Candy for his good behaviour, for the present. The other men avoided him, but no more attempts were made on his life. If anything, they were deferential. Whatever Brady had done, it worked. On the whole life was OK, thoughts of escape dwindled. It was good to come back to food and a warm woman in his bed at night.

Sometimes he missed the forest, the open sky, most he missed the comradery. Despite Brady's efforts, Los Vegas remained an ugly place of devastation. He looked out across the rubble won-dering if they might be persuaded to plant crops somewhere. He didn't think so with the raiders around, but the food stores wouldn't last forever, and it would take years before the animals revived in numbers ...

They ate alone as usual, Candy bringing the food. He slipped an arm around her waist nuzzling her neck. She seemed nervous about something he noticed, as he downed the stew.

"Come on Candy, out with it." He set his bowl aside, pulling her closer. "Don't tell me Brady wants to move me out again."

"No Vince, not that." Her eyes were teary. "It's not bad news, not really. I was going to tell you later."

"Tell me now."

"I ... I'm pregnant, Vince. I'm going to have your baby." She half laughed. Tears streamed down her cheeks. "Guess I wasn't totally infertile huh?" Vince was stunned. His world shook to its foundations. A child. His child ...

"You're pleased, aren't you?" she pleaded.

"Of course I am, Candy. It's just a bit of a shock." Complacency shattered, brain spinning, he took in the implications.

"You look worried ..."

"No, really, it's great news ..."

"You don't want it to grow up here ...?" She saw she'd hit the spot. "Once Brady knows she'll want it for her little kingdom. I don't want my son carrying a gun or even worse if it's a girl ..."

"No, Candy, I don't want that either. I'll get us away ..." Did he trust her? He'd have to trust her, she was having his kid. His thoughts flew to John, to Chad and Rat, to his long-gone brother. If he was going to be a father, to have another chance at family, he wanted to be like them. "I'll find a way Candy. I promise I will." He brought her hands to his lips, gently kissing the knuckles.

As Candy lay sleeping, his thoughts ran wild imagining a thousand scenarios. This changed everything! He must get them away. He racked his brains for a solution. The land around was desolate, even with a gun, could he find food ... and what of the raiders? No, to head inland would be disaster ... Maybe he could make it, but not with Candy in tow. The best way was by sea, but how? He remembered the mast they'd seen before Waterman took them to the larger vessel. He'd said the motor was gone, but perhaps the sails were OK. He could improvise a sail, not to cross the ocean, but to skirt the shore, head south ... but how could he get to it. What did he know about sailing anyway? The problems went round and round in his head but came to no solution. Finally sleep claimed him.

A gentle shaking awoke him. "Time to get going Vince or you'll miss breakfast ... You won't ... you won't tell anyone?"

"No way. They won't suspect till you start showing, maybe not even then ..."

"Guess that's one advantage." As he dressed his eyes drifted over her latest novel, tossed aside when he'd come home. Candy had the worst taste in books. Then a thought struck.

"Where do you get all these books, Candy?"

"Told you, in the library, what's left of it. Why? You can borrow some of mine if you wanna read."

"No thanks, but look, do you think you could see if they have any stuff about sailing there."

"Sailing?"

"Yeah, I was just thinking, if I knew how to sail maybe we could find a boat. Go out the back door so to speak." He wasn't about to tell her too much. "It's just a thought. I can't go rummaging around in there, but they'll take no notice if you do. Just don't let anyone see if you find something, cover it up with one of your novels."

"OK Vince. If you want, but it ain't no use, all the boats are wrecked."

"Maybe I could fix one up, head down south. Look, it's not like this everywhere Candy."

"I know, but I'm scared."

"Don't worry I'll take care of you." He lifted her face for a parting kiss as he headed out the door.

It was several days before Candy found something, even then it was not the best. The title *Tomorrow's Sunset* along with the bikini clad blonde languishing against the mast did not look promising. Still at least it was something.

"Thanks Candy, this will do for starters, but I need something more practical. Is there a reference section there?"

"D'know, the books are all in heaps, you just have to sort through."

"Maybe try a different pile or something. Wish I could come along, but I don't want anyone getting suspicious."

"I'll keep trying. Don't want to go too often."

"Right." Vince opened the book. It was every bit as bad as he feared. Still at least there were some helpful parts where the "darkly handsome Clint" taught the bikinied bimbo how to assist in the champion yacht race. It was nowhere near enough, but it was a start. Candy was vastly amused to see him pouring over the book taking notes. The big question was how to slip away to check out the vessel, even if he could reach it. A daytime trip would draw too much attention, he'd have to sneak out at night ...

"Be careful Vince."

"Don't worry I'll be back before sunrise." She nodded.

The lookout was drunk, Candy had slipped him a half empty bottle in exchange, so he thought, for keeping quiet about some clothes she'd pilfered from the laundry – Vince's idea.

Face and hands smeared with mud, a coil of rope over his shoulder, he slunk away into the night. Drawing close to the bay he hesitated, without Waterman could he be sure of the ground? How could he find the vessel without the row boat? Was there another way? One step at a time. First appraise the situation. He tested the earth with the branch. Each time it sank into squelching mud, only the path taken with Waterman seemed sound. It led solely to the planks and the rocks where he'd waited. He sat glumly at the water's edge. A momentary glimmer of moonlight caught something in the water. He peered into the shadows but could see nothing. He waited, cursing the clouds. Then, there it was, the rowboat, floatingly serenely, not ten yards away. John! It must have been John! A warm glow transfused his heart. Hope leapt. Memories flooded back. They'd waited, they'd left the boat for him, he knew it. If only ... He stopped himself. That part of his life was over, like his brother it was irretrievable.

The boat was there, caught in the eddies engulfing a ruined, half-submerged, willow, but how could he reach it. The rope wasn't long enough even if he could lasso something. Waterman had warned against swimming, anyway it was too shallow here, the mud would get him. He remembered the tide. It was coming in. Would high tide bring it closer or was it trapped in the branches? It would be worth the wait. What other option was there? He'd only have time to secure it before he had to get back. He'd come again somehow and go look for the sailboat. If only it would come!

He sat reminiscing. He remembered John's parting words, that if he didn't make it he'd be praying for him night and day. Vince had never prayed in his life, wasn't even sure exactly what he believed, but John did and that was a comfort.

"Hey John! Add a few for Candy and my child while you're at it," he whispered into the night wind.

He must have fallen asleep. He jerked awake as a spray of cold water soaked his leg. The tide was in, and there, there was the boat. He swung the loop eagerly over the water. It hit target but slipped away. There was nothing for it to catch on. Again and again he tried, merely succeeding in setting it spinning. So close but so far! There was only one thing for it. Slipping out of his clothes he edged into the water. It was deeper now. The cold struck his naked body like a knife. He swam a wary breaststroke, careful to keep arms and legs clear of the mud. He felt the lick of the current pushing towards the mud bound shore, but he was a strong swimmer. He had to make it before the cold took hold. Pulling himself over the side he slipped exhausted into the boat, cold sapping his strength. Finding the oars, stowed in the slime under the front bench, he pulled manfully for his former perch. The night wind chilled his chest and arms, his teeth began to chatter. It didn't matter, he had the boat. Pulling alongside he fished for the rope. It was hopelessly tangled. The lasso lay discarded on the rocks, holding the boat ring in one hand he reached. Yes, he had it. Quickly he tied his prize, retaining the end under one foot as he pulled on his clothes. He must get warm and fast. Mission accomplished, he groped around for the old root Waterman had secured it to ...

A scratching at the window woke Candy from a fitful sleep. *Vince, please God let it be Vince.* She opened the shutters and there he was, dazed and shaking, but alive. She helped him crawl over the sill half falling into the room.

"Vince ... you're like ice! What happened?"

"I'll be OK ... just need to get warmed up. I found something ... tell you later ... do you have any scotch?" She thrust a glass into his hand, helping him keep it steady. It frightened her to see him like this.

"Come, come to bed. I'll warm you up." She began to strip his damp clothes, rubbing life back into numb arms and legs. Taking off her robe she lay on top of him, the heat of her body slowly spreading to his own. He cracked a smile. Within seconds he was asleep.

He woke next morning to a raging headache. His limbs ached, and he felt decidedly unwell. Candy wasn't there, instead Mona stood before him, a bowl of soup in her hands.

"You look like death Vince. So, you're not impervious after all!" She laughed. "What's wrong, Candy been working you too hard?"

"Maybe ..."

"Looks like you got a fever. I got some meds. Here." She emptied out a couple of tablets and thrust them into his hand. "take them with the soup, OK?" Vince nodded obediently. She turned to go, then span around. "Look ..." she continued. "You were right, about Sully I mean. I ... we talked ... an' it's OK now. You were right ..." She made a quick exit as if the words might consume her.

Candy returned that evening, another bowl in hand. He'd slept well after the pills. His strength already returning.

"You're looking better," she smiled. "You scared me last night!"

"I found something, but I had the swim out to it."

"You ... found a boat?"

"Just a rowboat, not big enough to go far, but it could take us round the headland, down the coast a bit." He wasn't going to tell her about the other craft, not just yet.

It was several days before his strength was sufficient to dare another trip. The trick wouldn't work twice, besides alcohol was

66

running low since he'd taken up with Candy. She no longer felt inclined to "bargain" for it and he wasn't going to push her. He felt protective, especially now she was carrying his child. He'd just have to risk it.

He'd slipped out with little problem, the difficulty would be getting back in. At least he knew where the lookouts were posted ... He waited for the tide, going over the route in his head. Finally, the marker rock was covered. He slipped into the boat and pulled on the oars ...

There it was, just as he remembered. Pulling alongside he jabbed at the water with the oar, feeling the satisfying jolt of rock beneath. Tying the rope to the warped outer rail he slid aboard. It was hard to see in the moonlight. Groping, he found a small cabin, scarcely room for two bunks, but no matter, they'd not need much for a trip along the coast, just a few days supplies. The big question was, was it sound, and were the ropes and sails intact? The sheets were furled and as far as he could see undamaged. The ropes, though tangled, appeared to be sound. Water sludged around in the stern, where the tilt of the boat was lowest, but it could have been there some time. He wished Waterman were here, or that he could wait for low tide to see clearly what it was caught on. Would he be strong enough alone to prize it free?

Tacking back to the rowboat, he set off around the craft prodding with the oars to feel the depth. The blade caught in clinging mud as he rounded the back of the craft. Frantically he wrenched it free pulling hard on the oars, lest he become trapped. He noted the front lifted slightly with the waves, but the back held fast, doubtless trapped in mud. The boat was light, but there was no place safe to stand and lever it out, only the bow rested on firm ground. He racked his brains.

Tying the rope to the bow rail he pulled on the oars – nothing moved. He needed more power! A picture came to mind – Waterman wrestling to unsheathe the sail, the wind pulling them away to safety. He wet his finger, to gauge the direction of the wind. It gusted, bouncing off the encircling hills. It was chancy, with his limited navigational skills, but what other choice was there? Struggling in the darkness, he managed to raise the sail. Canvas snapped above him like thunderclaps. The boom swung, narrowly missing him as he dove to the deck. Grabbing the landing hook, he pushed at the muddy incline behind. It slid into the soft mud, then, miraculously, it hit something hard. Vince pushed as the boat shuddered. The pole slipped. Using all his strength he wrenched it free, probing again and again for the firm ground beneath. Then suddenly the boat broke free, toppling Vince into the stagnant water, the pole falling behind as the wind whipped the vessel around, the boom again flying free.

Leaping to his feet, he pulled in the sail, fighting the wind. He was not Waterman. The same power that freed the boat might fling him into some unseen peril beneath the waves. Grabbing the tiller, he used the momentum to steer into deeper water. Groping for the anchor, he let it down, surprised to find several yards pull out before it hit bottom. The craft calmed, and he was able to properly reef the sail. The wind was strong, and he didn't want it damaged.

The rowboat, bobbing at one side, had taken on a little water during the initial turmoil. Taking a wash bowl from the cabin he hasted to bail it out. Night was getting on.

Cold, exhausted and coated in slime, he neared the outskirts of Brady's territory. Choosing a smooth rock, he sent it splashing into one of the remaining seawater ponds to his left. Bullets burst through the surrounding bushes. Their eyes presently diverted, he sneaked forward keeping to cover ...

Candy was frantic as he rolled through the shutters.

"Vince, are you alright? I ..." He silenced her with a kiss, then held his finger to her mouth.

"I'm fine."

"But I heard gun fire ... I thought ... Boy you stink!"

"Just a diversion. Sorry about the smell, I fell in some stagnant water." Candy tilted her head in question – Vince was not the sort to fall into puddles. He grinned. "I fell when the boat we're gonna sail out of here pulled free!"

"A boat ... you mean the rowboat?"

"Not the rowboat, something bigger, something with sails and a small cabin." Candy lit up like a light bulb.

"We're going, we're really going, Vince?"

"You bet we are! But not a word yet. We'll need food and water, as much as we can carry ... and you'd better get these clothes washed for me or I may have some explaining to do – just as well you work in the laundry."

"We'll need clothes and things too Vince."

"We have to travel light, only what we can carry, and you shouldn't carry too much." He patted her belly, still showing little sign of the baby within. "One change of clothes only, and for God's sake make it practical. It's a long trek to the boat, and who knows where we'll end up. Some boots and pants would be good. You got anything like that?"

"No, but I can get it. There's a store of clothes and shoes and stuff. There were plenty for the taking after the big quakes." A thought re-emerged, from its long-buried silence.

"What did they do with the bodies?"

"I don't know, the guys took care of that. They just brought us the clothes and things to go through. Guess they must have buried them someplace."

"What about food? Is there a way to get food?"

"Can't help with that. The stores are all guarded."

"What about the kitchen? Maybe there's some stuff there?"

"I guess, but I never go there. You should ask Mona, you two were quite pally once." A frown creased the porcelain forehead as it always did when Mona was mentioned. Vince grabbed her shoulders spinning her towards him.

"Weren't ever anything between me and Mona. I told you that!"

"Show me again! But first get out of those filthy clothes and wash up a bit." Vince sighed inwardly, for all her charms he'd sooner have collapsed to sleep, it had been a long night ...

Worse was to come. Brady was in a foul mood having heard

the gunfire and found no one had been apprehended. She insisted on Vince standing guard that night to oversee operations. Able to catch only a few hours' sleep, his head was reeling, and he had trouble staying awake through the tedious night hours.

"Candy been keeping you up all night?" a voice cut in as Sully took over the second shift.

"She can be pretty demanding. Didn't know Brady was going to put me on an all-nighter."

"Getting old man!" The tone was sarcastic. Things had eased between them since Vince had dropped out of competition for Mona, but there was still an underlying tension. "Better watch out you don't nod off. Brady wouldn't like that." With a smirk he wriggled through the gap into the adjoining room. The lookout came out, yawning. Vince had no such relief.

Somehow he made it through, collapsing on the bed, asleep in seconds. Awaking to Candy's impatient nudging.

"You gonna sleep all day? I brought you some supper. Seems you slept through lunch." He looked up and smiled, his stomach was growling.

"Thanks Candy. I was so damn tired I could have slept for a week."

"I got you something!" She waved a volume triumphantly. "The Sailing Handbook" she trilled, "Reckon that ought to be more help, pretty dull reading though!"

"Candy you are an angel! Give it here!"

"I got clothes and boots too. I'm wearing them in." She waved a neatly shod foot for his inspection.

"That's my girl! Come give me a kiss." She launched herself into his arms for a quick kiss and cuddle.

"I even got a couple of cans." She added pulling away to extract them from under the bed.

"How in the hell ..."

"I told Mona I might be expecting, and she slipped me a couple."

"You what!" Vince froze. "I told you not to tell anyone!"

"Mona won't tell. She hates the whole 'breeding' thing. Be-

70

sides, I just said I might be … didn't say anything about plans and stuff."

"Thank God for that! No more though, the less people know the better."

"You mad at me Vince?" He pulled her close.

"No, not mad. I just want to keep you and the baby safe. If Mona asks, say it was a false alarm. Leave the food to me OK. I'll figure something cut. Maybe you could look out for something to store water in though. You seem to be doing great at scavenging."

"That's easy enough, we have plenty of buckets in the laundry."

"Something covered would be better, a big jerry can for example."

"OK, I'll look for one … I'm sorry Vince …" She slid a tentative finger over his cheek. Sometimes she reminded him of a child herself.

"It's OK, you were just trying to help, and you did get a couple of cans …"

Vince racked his brains over the next few days. Candy located some empty jerry cans, but food remined an enigma. The stores were heavily guarded, and, after the supposed intrusion, Brady was unlikely to shift his duties.

He was jolted from his thoughts as he caught movement among the bushes. He tapped his companion's arm.

"That bush, was it there before? I swear it moved." Len raised the automatic. "no, wait." Vince pushed it aside. "There may be more. If you go giving away our position they'll run for it."

The bush moved again. They peered into the darkness.

"There." Vince pointed again. "Let them get a bit closer so we've got a clear shot." A third party was spotted, slowly moving nearer. "OK, let 'em have it. You take the two on the right and I'll take the left and anything else that moves when we start up." Gunfire blazed.

"Damn missed him!" Vince swore, as a fourth figure made cover, slipping away into the darkness.

"We got three of them. Brady will be pleased. Let's not mention the fourth." Vince nodded. "Shall we go check 'em out?"

"Better wait on back up. They'll have heard the shooting. There could be more out there. Don't fancy walking into a trap. Course if you want to, go ahead." His companion shook his head vigorously.

Within minutes Mike appeared, followed by a couple of other guys.

"Did you get 'em?" he called.

"You bet we did, three of them!" Len whooped. "Vince said to wait for back up in case there's more out there."

"Vince would, wouldn't he?" Mike threw a withering glance.

"Tactics." Vince replied, "there might be a plan B, you never know." He said nothing of the fourth man, why make trouble for yourself.

"Pussy!" Mike intoned. "Come on, let's go see." Eager to ingratiate himself Len moved forward.

"I'll cover you." Vince said, steadying his gun on the opening.

"I'll let Brady know how brave you are." Mike spat at Vince's feet. He led the way, the others following. They'd covered half the distance when shots rang out. If the raider had an automatic he'd have got them all, even so he did well with a rifle, downing two men and winging Mike before Vince got him. There was no further firing. Mike appeared, fuming with anger, hand clutching a red drenched shoulder, arm limp.

"Come help us shift the bodies, if you're not still too pussy."

"My 'being pussy' as you put it, just saved your life. He was a crack shot that guy." Mike snarled but said no more.

Vince looked down at Len's glazed eyes. Stupid idiot, he should have listened. The other man lay likewise dead, shot through the head, Mike was lucky to have escaped with a busted shoulder. He silently applauded his adversary. They had perhaps had more in common. Maybe he should have let him finish them off, who was to know, but risky should one survive. No, he was a father now, or would be, better to play the game till the end.

He lifted Len over his shoulder. The other able-bodied guy

grasping Mike's downed comrade.

"You'll need to come back for the others." Mike ordered. "I'll keep an eye here."

"Why bother, we can bury them in the morning or just leave them to rot." Mike laughed. "Just do as you're told soldier boy .. and while you're at it, bring a few more guys."

Meeting a couple more reinforcements on the way, they passed on the bodies, instructing them to return and help. Mike was slumped against the wall, a pad of ripped cloth tied awkwardly over the wound.

"Take the others," he muttered. "Anyone else coming?"

"Yeah they're just dropping off our guys then they'll be here."

"That's good, I need to take care of this ... Vince, make sure someone's posted here, OK? Don't think we'll hear from them again tonight, but you never know."

Vince headed for the pile of debris behind which his previous opponent lay. He looked like a farmer. Beside him lay a hunting rifle, old and worn, such as Rat had carried. His heart lurched as he shouldered the body, following in the wake of his companion. Branching off, they headed in a different direction from before. Stumbling along in the darkness, he was surprised when they entered an old half ruined warehouse.

"Take 'em inside." The guard gestured. "Deal with them in the morning." Realisation dawned. Vince gagged. They were not going to bury them. This was a smoke house! He didn't need to see to the inner room to know what hung there, what he'd been eating all these months.

"What's wrong newbie, didn't you know?" his companion chuckled. "Can't be so damn finicky nowadays. We don't eat our own, only raiders." Vince tightened his lips. Don't react, don't let on, he told himself.

It all made sense – the missing bodies, the nightly stew, Mona's reaction about the kitchen. How had he not seen it? A chilling thought came to mind – John's guys finding the storage - that's why they set the trap, they'd wagered the canned goods in the hope of getting them all. His stomach turned. He had to get out of here.

He returned, shaken, to Candy's room. Brady had met them on the way back, furious at the loss of two men. She demanded the full story, before charging off to the lookout post. He wouldn't like to be in Mike's shoes ...

Candy too was shaken. "I heard the gunfire ... they brought back bodies ... I ... I thought ..."

"It's OK Candy," he dragged her to him, kissing her forehead. "I'm fine. It was Mike's fault. I warned him."

"Is he ..."

"No, sadly he's still alive, just a bit shot up. Two other guys paid the price for his stupidity. Would have been more had I not kept my head."

"Oh Vince, I'm so scared!"

"We're getting out of here, food or no food, OK? Can you get stuff ready for tomorrow night?" She nodded. He wondered if she knew about the meat, probably not. No use upsetting her, she was pretty emotional these days ...

8

He was woken early by a pounding at the door.

"Brady wants you," Tom growled. Generally, a stint on night shift was accompanied by a sleep-in till midday at least but the sun had hardly cleared the hills. Candy was already up and gone, leaving him a bowl of beans and hash for when he awoke. He looked at it longingly, but Brady wouldn't wait. Pulling on his clothes, he ran to follow Tom.

The atmosphere was intense. Mike was nowhere to be seen and Brady was in one of her moods.

"You're with me!" she snapped. "Seems you're the only one around here with an iota of sense!" This was unexpected. Vince picked up the proffered automatic, Mike's by the look of it, and scrambled after her. It seemed the dead raiders had done little to placate her.

All day he walked the tightrope of Brady's wrath, thankful to be on the right side of blame. Head throbbing, he longed to return to the peace of Candy's domain. Instead he was forced to accompany Brady to dinner. Gazing at the stew, his stomach turned. Others were watching he noticed, elbows prodding. He dare not balk. Somehow, he got it down, casually excusing himself after a few minutes, he ran to vomit into the hole that served as communal toilet.

"Can't take your medicine," a sarcastic voice intoned. "Fresh meat today, probably one of the ones you shot."

"What's it to you!" Vince spat, rounding on Sully.

"Me, nothing ... you're going soft that's all." Turning on his heel he moved away.

"Damn!" Vince hissed, just what he didn't want. Sully would have spread it all over by morning. He needed to head out tonight, once he could get clear of Brady. Brady however seemed in no hurry to dismiss him. Even after the evening's muted entertainments she continued his escort to her room. Bruno then departing, he turned to go likewise. Instead she seized his wrist.

"I didn't dismiss you!" She glared, then her gaze softened, like a cat playing with a mouse. "I have some extra duties in mind tonight. Prowess should be rewarded ... You won't be needing this." She slid the automatic from his shoulder propping it against the dressing table. Vince cursed inwardly. It didn't look like they'd be heading off tonight. He had to play along, she was in a dangerous mood. It wouldn't do to upset her.

"What you got in mind Brady?"

"I think you know." She rolled her eyes, sliding her finger down his chest. "What? You going soft Vince?" She gazed at his nether regions. "Maybe you been spending too long with Candy? She wearing you out?" Danger signals flashed in Vince's mind.

"Just tired, didn't sleep much. Give me a bit of time and I'll prove it." He raised a finger to stroke her cheek. Big mistake! Quick as a flash, she spun around. He felt a knife at his throat.

"Don't you ever, ever, touch me again!"

"I ... I'm sorry ... I thought you wanted ..."

"Well you thought wrong!" Pulling open the dressing room draw she drew out a length of looped cord. "This first, playboy! Big boys can be dangerous!"

"Whatever you want, Brady." Still grasping the knife, she slid the looped ends over his wrists pulling them tight. He could easily have overpowered her, but what about Candy? Brady wouldn't go down easy. The whole camp would come running. He might fight his way out but ... He found his hands securely tied around the bedpost as once before, but this time her intentions were different. Motioning him to lay down, she slid off his boots.

"Don't want to get the sheets dirty do we?" she mewed. Traveling upward, she smiled.

"Ah, that's better now. Knew you wouldn't disappoint." She opened his shirt button by button deliberately drawing it out before unhitching his belt.

"You know this could be a lot more fun if I could use my hands," he tried.

"Fun for who?"

"For you of course."

She laughed. "What, and have you finish before I'm good and ready. No, I like it this way."

"So, you gonna tease me all night, then leave me here?"

"Maybe ... or then again maybe not." She rubbed against him, capturing his lips, kissing deep and passionate, only to pull away, resuming her tantalising activities.

"God Brady. A man can only stand so much of that."

"That's precisely why you're tied." She laughed. It was going to be a long night!

He awoke from a dazed stupor. He felt for Candy. She wasn't there.

"I'm over here. Thought I'd spare you the cords. You were near exhausted, 'sides I got this." Brady indicated the automatic

76

perched beside her at the dressing table. It all came tumbling back, every agonising minute. Brady was a predator. He felt used, abused. He had some inkling of Mona's self-loathing. At least he couldn't get pregnant ... He desperately wanted to go but he had to play along, play Brady's games.

"Better get some food down, we got work to do." She motioned to a bowl of beans and hash. "Unless you prefer meat?" She raised an eyebrow. So, she knew, word travels fast.

"I'll go with this. Everyone has their preferences and eating someone I just shot isn't one of mine." No use skirting the issue. She laughed.

"So even you have your weak side huh? Better toughen up. Still, you got four last night, I guess I can overlook it."

"Len got two. Shame he never got to boast about it." Vince tried to switch the conversation.

"Mr humble huh?"

"The guy's dead, ought to at least give him credit."

"Len was stupid. He was warned. We can't afford to lose any more. That's why I'm putting you in charge of the lookouts. I don't understand why the raiders just keep coming. We've killed ten already by my count, and there weren't many to begin with."

"The guy I shot, the marksman, he looked more like a farmer. Maybe other folk are hungry too, looking for food ... or revenge," he muttered to himself. Perhaps they knew about the smoke house, maybe it wasn't only food they were after ...

He spent the day drilling tactics into the lookouts. Most of it was common sense, he didn't want to teach them too much, just enough to keep Brady off his back. If someone else were lost it would be on his head. He felt sympathy for these raiders, surely they could come to some agreement. If they shared the stores and worked the land together they could support them all, he remembered the farm. No use suggesting that to Brady, she'd never listen.

Candy appeared with the food in the early afternoon. She'd somehow persuaded Mona to let her bring it.

"Brady?" she whispered as she put his bowl before him. The

other two were sufficiently distant to risk a reply.

"Yeah, had me tied up all night, literally." He placed his wrists together on the bench. She looked worried.

"Is she mad at you?"

"No, just likes to play with guys ... Look it's still on, I just need to figure how to get us away safely. Keep the stuff together, but out of sight, OK?" She nodded. One of the guys came over and the conversation ceased.

"Nice piece that," he drooled watching Candy's retreating rear. "Got a thing for her, have you?"

"She's a good lay," Vince replied offhandedly.

"Alright for some. Word is you spent the night with Brady no less. Maybe you could pass Candy around a bit, share ..."

"My business who I sleep with! As for Candy, Brady decides that stuff, not me," Vince snapped, "and if I were you, I'd watch my mouth."

"OK, OK, just asking." He withdrew. Vince sighed, it was getting harder and harder to keep his relationship with Candy under wraps.

Again that night his presence was claimed, though to his relief Brady dispensed with the cords. Nonetheless bedding with Brady was like walking on a knife edge. She was demanding and aggressive, forcing him to play along. He hoped this would not become a regular feature of his life. He just needed one free night, but as night followed night, Brady seemed less and less inclined to dismiss him from her side. Even the lookout duties disappeared, and he found himself her constant bodyguard. He worried about Candy, some of the guys were hassling her now he was no longer in the picture. He noted she no longer took care of her appearance. Perhaps it was a ploy? He hoped she'd not started drinking again. He had to get them both away somehow.

The chance finally came. Brady unexpectedly dismissed him at her door. Bruno glared possessively before disappearing into the bedroom. Evidently this was part of the perks of the job. Vince had no complaints. Acting casual, he sauntered towards

Candy's room.

"Back to the honeypot is it?" Sully's sarcasm chimed in.

"Nowhere else to sleep."

"Well don't get any ideas about sneaking in on Mona while I'm on lookout."

"Believe me I just want a good night's sleep, Sully."

"Yeah, sure you're gonna get that with Candy?"

"Better than risking the dorm again ..."

"Well just be sure you keep on your own territory."

"Always do Sully." Vince moved on, leaving Sully to head for the lookout.

"Candy, it's me Vince." The door was locked, and it took a few minutes before it opened. Candy blinked.

"Vince? ..." Damn, she was drunk, this could wreck everything. God knows when he'd get another chance, he had to risk it.

"Get the stuff together we're going tonight!" She looked dazed.

"Thought you weren't ever coming back ... I thought ..."

"No Candy, no! I told you I'd come. This is the first chance I've had. You gotta sober up." He splashed her face, had her drink a bunch of water, opened the shutters to let in fresh air. It was no use.

"I'm sorry Vince ... I ..."

"Never mind. Look we have some time, try and sleep it off a bit, OK? We can't go yet anyway. Where's the stuff?"

"Under the bed ..."

Checking the packs, he came across the sailing book, flipping the pages, he watched her fall asleep, auburn curls draping her pillow. He'd grown fond of her. Night deepened, the book was too much to take in and he couldn't wait too long.

"Candy, Candy, we need to go." He shook her gently. It took a lot to wake her.

"Vince," she smiled, linking her hands behind his neck and stroking his hair.

"Not now, Candy. We need to go, remember?" A troubled

expression crossed her face. He pulled her upright, strapping on her boots - the pants and sweater she'd donned prior to sleeping. He took one last look through the shutters before dumping out the bags and slipping out. Candy followed stumbling.

"Quietly!" He hissed. She nodded. Slowly they edged away from the buildings. Vince knew the layout, where the lookouts would be posted. If only Candy hadn't gotten drunk. He had to watch her every step of the way, lest she stumble and make a noise.

So far so good. The lookouts were well behind now, and they could move freely. He'd have felt more at ease with a gun, but they were allocated only for duty hours. Candy was finding it hard going and had to stop frequently. He was impatient, knowing they needed to catch the tide right. At last the cove was in sight. Stopping off to fill the jerrycans, they headed down the slope toward it.

"Not far now Candy!" She picked up the pace, seeing the glimmer of water below. "Step where I step," he instructed as they retraced Waterman's path. He bent to take out the planks, still concealed in the bushes. Gunfire blasted! Candy fell, warmth spewing his hands as he caught her.

"No Bruno! He's mine!" a voice cut into the darkness. Brady!

"So, you thought you could sneak out on me did you. I always knew you couldn't be trusted. How do you think you got past the lookouts with that wreck making so much noise?" So, he'd been set up. After all this he'd failed ... "I'd like to make this more slow and painful, but I got stuff to do." She raised the automatic. Vince breathed deeply. So, it all ended here, all his hopes and planning had been for nothing.

Shots rang out, but not from Brady's gun. With a look of incredulity, she sank to the ground. Bruno spun, gun at the ready ... too late. He was mowed down in a hail of bullets. Vince looked around for his deliverer. Sully rose from the bushes.

"Sorry ... I wasn't fast enough." He glanced at Candy's prone form still cushioned in Vince's arms.

"But why? I don't understand. I thought you hated me?"

"Mona told me how you never went with her. It was deliberate wasn't it, you meant to let me win?" Vince nodded. "I owe you that, an' I pay my debts. I figured you felt the same about Candy as I did about Mona."

"She was pregnant, she was going to have my kid ..."

"I guessed that after she asked Mona for the cans. Thought you'd try to make a run for it. I tried to warn you to stay put tonight. I know Brady and her schemes. I figured she'd be watching."

"You're a lot smarter than I took you for Sully. What will you do now?"

"Say you killed them of course. Ain't no forensics these days who's to know. I just say I heard the shots and saw you escaping. That is what you're gonna do isn't it?"

"Yes, there's a boat. You want to come?"

"Me? No. I got Mona and my boy to think of. Things will change now Brady's gone."

"Look, Sully, you'll be short of men. Why not join with the raiders, share the food and plant a crop. The guy I shot was a farmer, maybe there are others. With Brady gone maybe they'd parley. If you keep feuding like this there'll be no one left." Sully smiled.

"See how things go with the others, but you got a point. Ain't the kind of life I want for my boy either. Look, I need to go, so do you. Sorry about Candy. I wasn't expecting Bruno to open fire."

"Think he was after me. You did your best and I'm thankful." Vince lifted Candy in his arms heading along the planks.

"You'd best leave her here. I'll make sure she has a good burial, no smokehouse and stuff. Mona hates that. Maybe if we can raise some crops, we can dispense with it and bury what's left. But meanwhile you don't have to worry about Candy, I'll take care of it, promise. You need to get going and fast." Sadly, Vince relinquished his burden to Sully, pausing to kiss her farewell. Then, unaccustomed tears welling, he grabbed the packs and jerry cans, dashing off across the planks. The water had risen and splashed at his feet. Gaining the rowboat, he waved farewell to Sully and to his past.

9

Grasping the rail, he swung the bags on board. The rowboat bobbed on the water as he leapt after them. Unhitching the rope, he hauled it round to the stern, securing it well. The shore was a shadowed darkness, there was no sign of Sully. He was free! Free, but at a price ... Candy was gone and with her the child. Alone in the darkness, a numbness enveloped him, hands working of their own accord, detached.

Pull yourself together! Focus! He upbraided himself. One false move and all would be lost ... All was lost ... Time to think later, he needed to rig the sail ... He had no idea of the contours of the land beneath, but better to go now under cover of darkness. Doubtless they'd be on their way and God help him if he drifted back into range after that. He knew there was deep water over by the cliff, best to follow Waterman's course. Fingers grasped the canvas, loosening the ties. The wind picked up, catching at the sail. The boat lurched as the boom swung. Clutching the tiller, he steered frantically toward the black silhouette of the cliffs, striving against a contrary wind, zig zagging an erratic course towards his goal. From there he could follow the coast south in search of a suitable landing place.

He was almost in position, the wind easing under the shelter of the cliff. He bent to free his foot from an entangling rope. Straightening, he was caught off guard. A fresh wind, rebounding from the bluff, filled the sail, swivelling the boom and sending him crashing against the rail. Pain exploded through his skull as the wind took possession of the vessel.

He awoke to a pounding head and queasy stomach. Disorientated, he sought to take in his surroundings. The boat, he was on the boat! Above, the sail bulged, as the craft surged over the water. Memory kicked in. Rising shakily to grip the rail, he looked around. There was no sign of the cliff, nothing but shadowed waves gleaming in the darkness. His heart pounded. How long had he been unconscious? Where was he? There was no way of knowing. Best wait for daybreak. He must be well out of range wherever he was? He'd have to risk it. His skull pounded as he crawled over to lower the anchor. Sinking back against the rail he rested for a moment before crawling into the cabin, dragging his pack behind. Better get some sleep ... hope it wasn't a concussion ...

Thirst woke him. He reached for the flask in the backpack pocket. His head was throbbing, the heave of the waves churned his stomach, but his vision seemed OK. Daylight filtered through the open door. Staggering to his feet, he leant on the frame to peer out. All around lay open water, not the slightest trace of land. Panic seized him. It's OK, it's OK, he told his beleaguered mind, the sun rises in the east, steer toward the sun and you'll sight land. He pulled up anchor. The wind seemed only too ready to oblige, though pulling toward what he judged to be north. Remembering the canyon and its vast waterfalls, he strove to adjust course with little success. The tiller was stiff, not responding properly.

A while later he realised. The sun was declining, not rising. He was heading south-west. Stupid idiot! He berated himself. It was no use cursing. He turned into the wind, pulling hard on the tiller. It suddenly loosened, the handle flowing back and forth with no effect. He raised it as far as he could. Between the ebb and flow of the waves he glimpsed what remained of the tiller – a mangled strip of broken metal clinging uselessly to the main rod. He recalled his frantic efforts to pull the boat free. The tiller must have been deeply entrenched ...

Without steering he was at the mercy of the south-west trade winds, blowing into the vastness of the Pacific Ocean. His head was pounding, he felt weak as a kitten. Even had he been at full strength, it was no use. Willing or not, he was being swept along in John's wake, but without the stores and water, without

Waterman's skills. Head spinning, he sank down against the rail. It was over, it was all over ...

"John if you're still praying for me, I could sure use one about now," he whispered.

Vince was awakened by a splatter of rain on his face. He felt dizzy, disorientated. The drops turned to a torrent. Rain – Water! Staggering into the cabin he emerged with the metal bowl. Wedging it into position, he watched the rain beat its rhythm on the base. He retired to the cabin, no sense getting wet, night was coming on.

While taking a last glance, to make sure the bowl was secure, he glimpsed a flash of light soaring across the heavens. Memories stirred. He recalled the lightning flash that delivered Chad and Bart, the globes that spun through the air during the quakes and meteor showers, but most he remembered his encounter with the being inside the light. No guns, it had said, no more killing ... What had he been party to since then? ... The first time on the cliff top was to save John's band, but the others ... the others had been to save his own hide ... guilt and condemnation overwhelmed him.

"Chad you were wrong about me. Why did you plead for me? I just reverted to type," he called to the wind ...

A still, small, voice echoed within. He'd abhorred his role, had to fake acquiescence ... Had something changed? Had he changed? He remembered the farmer he'd shot, there'd been no pleasure, no satisfaction, just a deep sadness at the necessity ...

"But you killed him! Maybe you felt bad, but you killed him!" guilt replied. He pictured the famished form, blood oozing softly, other pictures came. He raised his arms, hands flapping hopelessly at the images crowding his beleaguered mind. Was "God", or whatever force it was behind the messengers, judging him? He'd lost Candy and the child, now he was adrift on the ocean. The slow, painful death he had avoided by playing Brady's games had come upon him in a different form ...

Rain continued its mocking song, beating on the cabin roof,

splashing into the bowl outside. His stomach growled. He had Candy's tins. May as well eat one, one now and one tomorrow, then ... Then maybe he'd end it, why draw things out? Cheat God, take his own life ... But perhaps, perhaps there'd be a boat, maybe he'd be rescued? Rescued? There's hardly anyone left alive on the planet and you think a boat will come sailing by? It was impossible ... but then many things had been impossible ... He remembered John's quiet faith. "God would supply," he'd said, and he had. Not just one boat but hundreds, and Waterman, what kind of miracle had Waterman been? But that was John. John was a good man, kind, compassionate, different to him.

But John is praying for you ... Hope stirred for a moment. Sitting up, his hand brushed against his leg, the leg that had been full of gangrene, that any doctor would have amputated, the leg whole, healthy, unscarred. Chad had pleaded for his life, not his leg, the leg was a gift. No one had interceded for that. Perhaps Chad and John were not the only ones who cared? Perhaps ... perhaps ...

Swinging off the bunk he rummaged for the cans and the opener. The water should be boiled. A small burner swung suspended on top of the cupboard. Inside were two pots, one inside the other, and a small frying pan, tin plates and mugs two of each, basic, but sufficient. He had what he needed for right now, but what about tomorrow? What about a week from now, a month?

There was nothing he could do, nothing. He was adrift in the midst of the ocean, his situation impossible. Even were there no storms, even should he chance upon land, it would take weeks to cross the Pacific. He was alone at the mercy of God, could it be "God" would preserve him somehow, or was this his judgement. Was there someone out there who cared, as Chad had cared, as John had cared? He would put it to the test.

His stomach growled in direct proportion to the recovery of his head. It had been days since he devoured the second can. Fresh water he had from intermittent rainstorms, but food was another matter. His joyous find of a small fishing line had yielded no results. He was no Waterman. He didn't know the ocean or the fish. Perhaps all the fish were dead too. Waterman had said they were reviving, but the ocean was vast, if there were fish, where would they be? Even if he knew, he had no means of steering the vessel.

His thoughts turned to the ancient fishermen. He'd heard the story as a child. "Cast your nets on the other side," Peter had been told. He'd even tried it a few times in some inane hope of procuring a miracle to ease his aching stomach. Nothing happened. How long could a man go without food? Starvation was a slow process. His body, lean and well-muscled as it was, held little in the way of reserves. Perhaps he might last the trip, but would he be strong enough to ply the oars of the rowboat or swim for land if opportunity arose? Probably not.

He gazed down at the sailing manual that had become his only recreation aside from a pocket Bible and cookbook he'd found waterlogged in a draw and dried out. Minus the tiller, there was little enough he could apply in the way of sailing. The cookbook was a torture. He leafed randomly through the wrinkled pages of the pocket Bible tilting it toward the waning light, remembering Rat's interest in the book of revelations. He paused. He'd be out here a long time, maybe start at the beginning? Genesis … his eyes lit on a verse, "and the spirit of God moved over the face of the waters". Here, surrounded by the vastness of the ocean, he pondered the words … The sun was setting, tinging the horizon to misty red, its fire doused by the eternal ocean. It was beautiful out here sometimes … Too dark to read, he lay on deck taking in the vast magnificence, a speck floating in a universe of water. He looked up at the blanket of stars, picking out the few he knew from old navigation skills. Space engulfed him, embalming him in surreal perspective. Nothing mattered, he didn't matter, the heavens and the earth, the ocean, would continue, held in some infinite power beyond his understanding.

His ears attuned to the rhythmic splash of the keel against the waves, the sound of the sails dancing with the wind in their nightly rituals. Glancing behind he noticed a gleam on the waves. Rising, he looked over the stern rail. A luminous trail spread behind him, phosphorous on the waters. He gazed enthralled at the beauty of it all. If a man must die then better so under the open sky, at peace with the world around him. It didn't matter, he decided. He would live, or he would die, but every day the demons of his past receded, engulfed by the immensity surrounding him. Nightmares had subsided. He dreamed of stars and water and sometimes of Chad. Yawning he contemplated sleep, but no, not yet, he would take it in a while longer, be at peace with nature ... surrender ...

"I'm yours, whatever you want to do with me!" he bellowed to the heavens. Was "God" listening? It was all so much bigger than him. No matter how much he messed up, it would continue, serene, infinite, beyond his understanding. He lay upon the womb of water from which life had begun. What must it have been like back then he pondered ...? At last he retreated to the cabin, fatigue overcoming his aching belly.

He was awoken by a strange, sploshing sound as something hit the deck,. Rushing to the door, he could scarce believe his eyes. Something was leaping over the boat, a whole bunch of somethings. His eye caught the gleam of fins like tiny sails catching the moonlight. Fish! Flying fish! Splat, another, then another, missed their aim to land squirming on the deck. He'd heard tales, but dismissed them as old fisherman's yarns, but there they were. He rushed to grab them, banging them against the wall to bring a quick end to their struggles. The last few sploshed into the waves on the far side of the boat and they were gone, skimming over the ocean, but he had four. Food at last! A thought wondered through his mind. Had "the fisherman" sent them? Was he caring for him as he'd cared for John? His heart secretly warmed at the thought ...

Day broke, his belly no longer empty, the remaining three fish hanging to dry. He smiled. Reaching for the pocket Bible, disregarding Genesis for the present, he thumbed through to the New Testament ...

Li Hua looked out over the ocean, tears welling. She felt so alone. Before the children she must keep her sunny countenance, but here, alone among the ocean waves, she could grieve. The wounds refused to heal. Inside was an emptiness nothing could fill, even the love and affection of the children. Crops were growing well, the rice now accompanied by vegetables, sweet potatoes, even sugar cane. Banana and pineapple were once more there for the picking, the children lacked nothing. They slept under the stars or in the simple lean-tos they had erected on the high ground near the beach. She'd moved them away from the ruins, from the ghosts and memories that plagued them all. The children were young. Here in the beauty and wonder of nature they would have the chance to grow strong, leave behind the shadows, for her it was not so easy ...

10

Another day alone on the ocean. He had to put it to the test. One of the dried fish remained, it alone would not last him the rest of the journey. Shaving off a tiny segment he baited the hook, heart pounding within him. Had the fish been co-incidental? The sail hung limp. His journey postponed at the wind's pleasure. He trailed three lines over the keel of the boat. Watching was an agony, instead he seized the tattered book. He was wading through the old testament. Though laced with familiar stories, it was more tedious than the new, some parts he'd skipped altogether. His interest revived in the stories of David, the lion and bear, Goliath etc. then petered out again at a vast succession of kings, most of them bad. He was about to give up on it when his eyes caught a line. "The ravens brought him bread and meat ..." What was this about? He back tracked to catch the story – Elijah, the drought, running from the king, hiding by the brook, and there it was ... "The ravens brought him bread and meat in the morning and bread and meat in the evening: and he drank from the brook."

"God" had done it before, he could do it again? But Elijah had been God's man, doing God's business, Vince was not ... Yet there had been the sailfish, his leg ... He stroked his thigh as he often did these days. He watched the birds that sometimes circled above, none seemed bent on a mission of mercy ...

One of the lines began to twitch. Cautiously he hauled it in. Silver scales splashed against the waves. It was not big, but sufficient for a good supper. Perhaps he was not worthy of ravens on a heavenly mission ... but God, it seemed, was prepared to keep him alive by more simple means. Stowing the fish, he re baited the hook, this time with fresh meat. A few hours provided several more to be hung and dried – fresh meat worked better. As the sun grew low in the west a breeze began, he let out the sail and proceeded to cook supper.

Vince lay on deck looking up at the stars, his belly appeased. It was a clear night. He hoped it would rain soon, water was getting short and a film of salt water, combined with the increasing heat, had rubbed him raw. He envisioned standing in the flow of a heavy tropical downpour. There'd been no squalls, for which he was thankful. Perhaps it was a part of this new order of things, he could remember no storms of any kind on their trek west or in Las Vegas. The heat was stifling now. His shirt he'd long abandoned, indeed a good part of the day he wore only boxers – who was there to see? Even so the waistband had formed a band of raw speckled flesh beset by heat rash and irritated by the ever-present salt. Finally, sick of the irritation, he abandoned them also, luxuriating in the freedom. Perhaps Adam felt like this he pondered, naked, alone, except for God. Was God truly with him or was it all coincidence he wondered? He rubbed his leg, it was reassuring ...

Weeks had passed, alone on the vastness of the ocean, just him and the presence that somehow sustained him with just enough to keep body and soul alive. His gums were sore, and he felt increasingly lethargic. Early signs of scurvy, scourge of ancient sailors. There'd been little enough vitamin C in his winter diet and now none for weeks. He looked at the notches – forty-seven days. Surely he must be nearing land soon? What if he was too far south, missing China and south-east Asia, heading toward the Indian Ocean? What if they were no longer there, if the coastline had changed like the US? He pushed the thought from his mind. Something, someone, had kept him all this way. Why preserve him for nothing? He reached for the Bible and began to read. It was familiar now, a source of comfort. The end spoke of new beginnings, a new world after the devastations he'd been party to. It brought back the remembrance of Rat, of his self-conscious admission of the passage in Revelation, of their comradery. If only he'd stayed with Rat and the others. If only he'd made it to the boat with John, if only Sully had been quicker and Candy hadn't died ...

But perhaps ... perhaps he had a destiny of his own. Maybe there was a place for him somewhere out there beyond the Pacific ...

Days passed in increasing stupor. Rain beat down in rhythmic patterns, he listened to it ebb away, too weak to place the bowl to capture it, barely able to refill the flask from the diminished water jug. Dreams and reality intermingled engulfed in sea and tide.

The ocean ranged before him, vast, infinite. He raised his arms in familiar motion as he swept upward. He wanted to gain altitude but seemed bound by the sea, pulling him earthward ... A sea of light and laughing faces invaded. Children, dark, slanted eyes wrinkling in amusement beneath wet, black hair. Curious fingers poked at his beard, voices whispered and giggled, like bubbling creatures of the water ...

A voice rang out, chasing the faces away. A mirage swam before his eyes, a sea spirit, wet and beautiful, eyes dark as night, water dripping from her ebony braid. Something light and airy swept through the air. She was trying to lift his head.

He struggled, confused, resisting. A boy leant forward, white teeth grinning against dusky skin, thrusting a pillow beneath his head and shoulders. There was something against his mouth, water sloshing against his lips. He gulped greedily. Strange utterances rang out, short and tonal. The water was removed.

11

"Can you sit up?" the voice came from a great distance.

"I ... I ..."

"Don't try to speak ... Save your strength." Sounds washed over him unheeded, like ocean waves.

"Fruit ...?" He yelled ... but all that came forth was a strangled sound. Words reverberated, half speech, half strangled song. The boy's face disappeared. The room swam.

"Who ...?"

"Don't talk. drink a little more." A cup was raised to his mouth. He took a few gulps and began to gag. "Slowly, a bit at a time,' the goddess coaxed. He glimpsed his flask, it stood full of water Was this real? What were they doing on the boat? ... The stars were circling above, lights flashing across the sky ... Candy whispered ... dreams blended.

His eyes flickered open as consciousness returned. There was no sign of the woman, or the laughing faces, but his flask and a bowl of fruit stood beside him. Easing onto his side he reached for them. There was a scampering of feet as a voice called out. A head peered round the door, the boy again. Was it a dream? The water seemed real enough, not cool but refreshing. The boy moved to help steady the flask. Vince was weak as a kitten. He drank greedily, gagging on the flow. The boy pulled it away shouting and gesticulating. There was a splashing noise and the "goddess" appeared, again drenched from the sea, but seeming more human. She smiled.

"You look a little better. Hai brought the fruit, but you were sleeping."

"How did you ... get here?" His voice came as a croak soon disappearing altogether.

"We swam. Don't try and talk. You're still very weak." The boy said something.

"He says you drink too fast." She smiled. "Your mouth is swollen, just take sips, a bit at a time."

"How ..."

"You are close to shore," she anticipated him. "We couldn't get the boat around the rocks and you're too heavy for us to carry into the little boat." The boy again said something. "The steering is broken," she translated. Vince nodded, wanting to explain, wanting to ask more, but she hushed him. "You need to rest. Save your strength to eat and drink." She started to peel a banana. He shook his head.

"Scurvy ..." Obviously she didn't understand. He pointed to the mango. She shrugged, but began to peel it, edging tiny slivers between his parched lips. It stung, and his gums and teeth hurt but he managed to get some down followed by a few more sips of water. Patiently she renewed the process coaxing him till he once more faded into oblivion.

He woke to the rhythm of raindrops pounding on the roof above. He was alone. Night breezes blew rain cooled air into the cabin, sweet and refreshing. Had it been a dream? He reached, fumbling in the darkness for the flask. Raising it to his lips, he felt the sweet taste of water. It was not a dream. It went down more easily, but he schooled himself to take it slow. He noticed the outline of a bowl. Carefully he pulled it to him, feeling inside the soft fleshy pulp. They'd left mango ...

He must have dozed again for now the sun was shining. His attempts to sit up were met by the grinning face he'd seen in his dream. The boy came forward to help, pulling on his shoulders and moving the pillow to a better position. He smiled, thrusting a bowl of watery rice into his hands, motioning him to eat. It looked disgusting. Vince shook his head.

"Fruit ... I need fruit." His voice was returning, but the boy clearly didn't understand. Vince looked for the old bowl, but it was gone. The boy thrust the rice towards him. Again, he shook his head pushing it away. Eventually, after several efforts, the boy left in a huff to sulk on deck. It was a while before the woman came, dripping wet as before. The boy was gesticulating and speaking angrily. Vince was in the doghouse it seemed. He tried to raise his voice to call but it came with only a croaking whisper.

"It seems you didn't appreciate the congee Hai made you," she smiled.

"I need fruit ... Scurvy ... I have scurvy ..."

"What is scurvy? I never heard of it."

"No vitamin C ... you get sick ... die." Vince gasped.

"Ah! I see." Eyebrows raised, she turned to talk once more to the boy. There was a splash. "OK Hai will bring more mangos. Mangos are best, yes?"

"Yes, mango ... more vitamins."

"Hai was very insulted. They took a long time to make congee for you. When he got sick his mother always made him congee. It's a Chinese thing."

"You are Chinese?"

"No, Hai is. I'm Tung fan chi." She laughed. "You don't know what that is, right?" He shook his head. "You are close to Hualien, or what's left of it." Hualien also meant nothing to Vince ...

"Indonesia?" he questioned. She laughed.

"This is Formosa, Taiwan ... the east coast. You Americans don't know geography."

He decided to avoid any more derogatory comments. Besides it was an effort to talk. She popped outside bringing a bottle from which she refilled his flask, then used a little of the fresh water to wipe his face and sticky hands.

"You're all covered in juice, even the sheet is sticky." she chuckled, "If you go on eating just mango you are going to get the runs. Maybe you should try some of Hai's congee or at least a banana. I told him to bring both. We have pineapple also, but your mouth is too sore right now."

"Banana." He couldn't face the thought of the congee. He

grabbed her hand as she went to leave. "Thankyou ..." he muttered. She snatched it away, flustered.

"No thanks needed."

His strength was returning. He'd discovered the congee not as bad as he'd imagined, though he still preferred the bowls of rice and vegetables that appeared each evening. His teeth and gums had recovered sufficiently to eat a more balanced diet now, for which he was relieved. The warning of loose bowels had been fulfilled in an embarrassing episode. Unable to make the porta-potty alone, he'd been forced to accept Hai's help. Hai seemed to find it most amusing, the word "congee" much in evidence.

Vince and his self-appointed guardian were slowly building a relationship of sorts, using a few English or Chinese words and a large diversity of mime. It was good to have company of any sort after the long time alone on the ocean. He sensed a need in Hai, different perhaps, but equally intense. The woman, from what he could discern, was busy. He had so many unanswered questions and was impatient to explore his new domain. Soon he would be able to make it into the boat, but would they be able to row him ashore?

His legs were shaky as he staggered to the doorway. Dawn was breaking over the sea. Beyond the surrounding rocks he traced the outline of the shore, palm trees silhouetted against a lightening sky. Not far off ... He could have swum it easily in days past. Just a small stretch of water between him and land ...

Hai woke from his deskside slumbers, grinning to see Vince standing unaided. He wasn't always there. He must swim back and forth Vince supposed. Hai pointed over the water.

"Hualien!" he announced. Vince smiled and staggered back to bed. There was a splash outside.

The woman had come. He watched as she approached taking in the lithe figure and flawless features. Perfection, and definitely human. He wondered if she were taken. Were those faces he'd seen her children?

She saw him looking, it made her angry. He was like all the rest. Perhaps she should have left him to die ...

"Hai said you can walk now. Can you make it into the boat?" She bit her tongue, doubts besetting her. Did she really want to bring him ashore?

"Not yet, tomorrow maybe. I'm still pretty weak. Not sure I'd make it over the rail ... probably end up in the water." He smiled depreciatingly, cursing his luck. He was a mess, didn't like to be seen like this.

"Can you swim?"

"Normally I could swim it easily ... but now ..." he muttered under his breath. "It seems from what I could make out from Hai you are busy farming? I'll be strong enough to help soon.' He didn't like being dependant, wanted to make sure they knew he could pull his weight. "You've been feeding me, I owe you ...'

"We're harvesting the rice."

He sensed a coolness in her voice, an apprehension. His affirmations only seemed to make her more uneasy. He changed tack.

"Please, tell me about this place. I have so many questions. I know nothing about Taiwan."

"It's a large island, off the coast of China."

"Part of China?"

She was obviously affronted. "Part of China! No! The Chinese came here many years ago. Chiang Kia Sheck and his Han nationalists. Many, many, came after Mao defeated them ... but it is our island. My people, we kept to ourselves up in the mountains. They looked down on us, the Han with their cities, but they left us in peace for the most part. Then the World Government took over. They ransacked the villages, tried to force us all to register, become part of their system ..." Her eyes clouded with tears.

"But you rebelled?"

"Not rebelled. My people could not fight their guns and planes. We hid, we found refuge in our mountains." Her chin tilted defiantly. How beautiful she was ... Vince reached to take her hand. She recoiled. He desperately wanted to reassure her

"I'm not government. I ran and hid too, tried to help those hiding. I'll help you too, if you let me."

"How do I know I can trust you? I saw when I washed your hands ... you carry the mark, but you're not dead ... Si wan said God destroyed everyone who had the mark, but you, you survived?"

"I dug it out when we took to the wilderness. We all did. See?" He held out his hand again, slowly this time. Hesitantly she examined it. "It's just a scar, nothing in there," he continued. "Me and Chad, and Rat and the others we fought against the government troops." She withdrew her hand rapidly, fear flashing in her eyes.

"You fight? You kill?"

"There were other folks out in the wilderness, we tried to protect them." He knew it wasn't really true, not for himself, but there was truth in it, true for Chad, for Rat. "But I'm not going to hurt you or Hai, or anyone else unless they try to hurt you guys OK?" She nodded, still hesitant.

"Where were you going? We can help you fix the boat. You can find tools and things in the old city." She wanted rid of him ...

"I was escaping from some evil men in the US, gangsters. They shot Candy, my woman, then the rudder broke and I was washed out to sea."

"You came from the US in that boat. How? It's impossible!"

He hesitated. "God kept me." The words sounded strange. It was the first time he'd confessed it to anyone, even himself. "I think He brought me here to help you and Hai. Are there others? You mentioned Si wan?"

"Si wan, he died." Tears welled. Her husband, brother?

"Please, let me help. I don't want to be alone anymore ..." his voice broke as he struggled for control. "You don't know what it's like day after day ..." He stopped before the floodgates broke.

"We'll help you come ashore, find tools to fix your boat, but you need to understand, I am not part of the deal!" The eyes flared. "If you lay one hand on me, I'll kill you!"

"Agreed." Vince was taken back by her vehemence. They must

have raped her, God damn them. She turned to go.

"I'll come back tomorrow, if you feel strong enough for the trip. Hai will bring some clothes."

"I have a shirt in the bag, but some shorts would be good. It's so hot."

"Plenty of clothes in the old city. Hai will bring some. Maybe a T shirt might be better too?" Vince nodded. He'd discovered a pair of boxers, washed and neatly folded by the bed soon after the porta-potty incident and assumed it had been Hai, but perhaps not. The rash had healed and, wishing to avoid future embarrassment, he'd donned them.

They sat on deck, Vince's back propped against the rail, eating the familiar rice and vegetables. Hai had tried to teach him to use chopsticks, but he preferred the china spoon.

It was good to be outside the cabin. The setting sun bathed the hills in splendour. Near the trees he could make out the shape of rough buildings. Maybe there were more people living here? Why had a man not come in that case? The woman spoke English, but what man, would send a woman alone on such errands. Perhaps there were only women and children left as John had said? He hoped there was another, like the English speaking one, but more amenable. He realised he didn't even know her name.

He turned, pointing first to Hai. "Hai," then, indicating himself, "Vince." "Woman?" His hands depicted the age-old shape, then pointed to the shore and made swimming motions. Hai chuckled.

"Li Hua." He mimed picking a flower and smelling the perfume. Perhaps she was named for a flower, or perhaps Hai had misunderstood?

They sat companionably as the sun reclined. Vince wondered about Hai. Most probably an orphan, or perhaps Li Hua's son? Asian women were slower to age, yet it seemed unlikely. He pointed to Hai and folded his arms as if rocking a child.

"Li Hua?" He questioned. Hai laughed, shaking his head vigorously. He pointed to the boat then stood arms bent, flexing the ropes of muscle slowly forming. He repeated the motions again and again adding strange additions. Vince could understand nothing. It was often that way. Finally, Hai sat down exasperated. Vince chuckled, pulling him into a playful headlock, ruffling his hair as he'd once done another boy, long ago, before Chad, before the army … Hai squirmed and giggled. Then, pulling free, he gazed boldly into Vince's eyes pointing questioningly first at Vince's chest and then his own. That Vince understood. Hugging him, he let the tears fall just a little.

She appeared the following afternoon. They saw her coming, arms gliding smoothly through the waves. She was startled to see Vince sitting on deck.

"Li Hua?" he announced. She nodded, scaling the guard rail. His eyes wandered to the sodden shirt. Kicking himself, he averted his gaze. Hai circumvented disaster as he came to give her a hand up, talking excitedly. She frowned.

"Hai seems to think you're going to be his new father. I told him he probably misunderstood."

"Father?" Vince questioned. "I was thinking big brother. I don't think I'd fill a father role so well, at least not yet." She translated for an anxious looking Hai. He thought for a moment then nodded, smiling.

"I lost my brother a long time ago," Vince explained.

Her face clouded. "You have lost a lot of people?"

"We all have."

"Do you think you can make it into the boat?"

"I can make it in if you guys can row, don't think I'd be much use just now."

"I'm not so good, but Hai can row. He's stronger than he looks." She tapped Hai's arm so he would know what she was saying. "He grew up on boats. He's hoping we can fix this one so he can go fishing." That went some way to explaining last night's charade.

"He's not yours then?"

"No, I can't have children. He's my little brother too." She translated for Hai.

"Tell him we'll fix the boat and he can teach me to sail better." Hai nodded enthusiastically.

"So, let's try to get you into the little boat then ..."

Hai clambered down like a monkey, but it was all Vince could do to edge slowly over the rail, and Li Hua had to help lower him down. Even then he landed in a heap that almost overturned the boat.

"Sorry," Vince muttered. Hai laughed, chattering something about "de de."

"He says you are the little brother!" Li Hua laughed.

"Maybe he's right for now, but tell him I'll get even." He ruffled Hai's hair as the boy reached for the oars.

The going was a little slow with their combined weight and only Hai to ply the blades, none the less, he set his mouth determinedly and pulled for shore. She was right, he was stronger than he looked.

"Do you have fresh water nearby, somewhere I could bathe?" Vince asked.

"A stream comes down over there," she pointed. "There's a pool a little further off when you are stronger."

"Even a stream would be great right now. I saw lots of huts on the beach, are there many people living here?"

"Not many." She shot a warning glance to Hai. "They are all away getting in the rice harvest."

Hai looked annoyed. Something was going on, something she didn't want him to know.

As it turned out Vince barely made it off the boat and into the small lean-to they had prepared for him. Washing would have to wait. At least he'd made it ashore. Hai brought him food and set the flask beside him, returning with his own bowl. They ate in companionable silence, Hai sensing his fatigue. He fell asleep almost immediately.

12

Morning dawned, creeping across the ocean, invading his dreams. The sounds were different, his bed strangely still? – He remembered. Opening sleepy eyes, he took in the sunrise, the gleaming sand. Against all odds he'd made it.

"Thank you! Thank you!" he whispered to the presence that had somehow brought him here. Wobbling slightly, he emerged to look around. Trees whispered in ocean breezes, not pine, not elm, but palm. He glimpsed coconuts. Somewhere bananas and mangos grew, and pineapples she'd said. It was paradise! Sitting cross legged in the sand he took in the vista, listened to the pounding of the waves. There was no sign of Hai. He wondered where he slept. He was too weak to go looking. Hai would come.

Sure enough, not long after, Hai emerged from the trees, a bowl of rice in his hand and a large bunch of bananas slung by a string over his shoulder. They were smaller, a different kind than Vince had seen before, but delicious. Hai smiled, thrusting the bowl into Vince's hand and helping himself to one of the bananas. Eat, get strong, he mimed. Vince had no trouble cooperating, his appetite had returned, a good sign ...

Never had water felt so good! He sat, legs semi-emerged, splashing water over his body and occasionally at Hai. It didn't matter that he was naked, there was no one to see, only him and Hai and they were brothers. Hai did likewise (though retaining his shorts) laughing and splashing Vince in retaliation. Neither saw Li Hua approach. She smiled seeing them enjoying the water.

"Men never grow up!" she teased. Vince splashed water at her. She stepped back. "So, you made it to the stream," she continued. "I brought some clean clothes just in case." She set a pair of faded shorts and a T shirt down on the sand. "Should have left your boxers on. Clothes dry quickly here, but then you seem to have a thing about going naked."

Vince coloured slightly, feeling strangely awkward. "I didn t know you'd be coming. There was only me and Hai and I wanted to get properly clean."

"Then you'd better wash these too or you'll get dirty again putting them on." She threw the offending boxers into the stream and he scrambled to get them lest they float into the ocean. Hai laughed and said something in Chinese. She didn't interpret.

"Don't overdo it. You'll need to head back to the lean to before the sun heats up." She spoke to Hai who looked a little downcast but began to gather Vince's clothes for the walk back. It wasn't far, but she was right, the sun was exhausting. Even with the ocean breezes the land was hotter.

For the next few days he mostly ate and slept. Sometimes Hai was there, sometimes not. He took advantage of their time together to learn a few words of Chinese, which Hai seemed eager to teach, requiring the English word in return. Hai was definitely the better scholar.

Li Hua would come each evening to see if there were anything he needed, but his inquiries were met only with the response that he had been very sick and needed to rest. There'd been no sign of the other occupants, though Vince found traces of children in some of the huts he'd explored. There were no tools though, nothing with which he could engage himself. His strength was quickly returning and, aside from needing a nap in the heat of the day, (something even the energetic Hai frequently did) he felt able to work. Li Hua remained elusive, suggesting, when pressed, that they might try to bring the boat ashore. He supposed she was still hoping to get rid of him.

One morning, waking early enough to see Hai set off, frustrated for answers, he followed. Cover was abundant and Hai unsuspecting. The major difficulty was keeping him in sight. Familiar with the ragged trails, Hai moved swiftly, Vince less so. He'd almost given up when voices wafted through the undergrowth, children's voices. Vince remembered the visions on the boat. There had been children. Perhaps they also had been real, Hai's friends maybe? He edged forward peering between giant foliage.

There were children everywhere, squatting on the ground, bowls and chopsticks rattling as breakfast was consumed! He saw Hai standing in line before a large pot from which Li Hua stood ladling out rice. Where were the adults? Had they gone off to the fields already? Hai was nearing the pot. Vince rapidly retraced his steps. He barely made it.

Hai grinned to see him up and around. Setting the rice bowls before them, he made eager motions with his hands and arms – the sea, rowing … He was eager to follow through on Li Hua's suggestion. Vince nodded, why not? He indicated the food, then his belly, finally folding hands beneath his head. Hai pointed to the sun – hot – tired. Vince nodded. Had he not followed Hai he'd have set off straight away, but he'd best rest a little first.

It was in fact early evening when they finally set out for the boat. Vince, having learnt from his escapades with Waterman, realised the task was better attempted at high tide when the boat could be brought further up the beach.

Hai took the first shift, rowing out to the rocks, conserving Vince's strength. Clambering aboard Vince noted the anchor had been dropped, a fact eluded in his former daze. He pointed to Hai questioningly. Hai nodded, blowing and making wave motions. Vince smiled giving the universal thumbs up signal. Both wind and tide would be in their favour once round the arm of the rocks, but it took all Vince's recovering strength, to drag the vessel back into the open sea. Hai, left on board with "instructions" to lower anchor if they couldn't make it out, waved exuberantly as they cleared the last of the rocks, flexing arms and pointing to Vince. His smile dimmed as he saw him sag forward against the paddles. Diving in he clambered aboard the rowboat, grabbing the oars. Thankfully with tide and wind now in his favour he was able to successfully tow the boat shoreward. Vince was thankful for the rest, and for Hai's handling of the landing, rowing in sync with the waves. As they drew close, he saw Li Hua appear, calling and waving hands.

Feeling a sudden, contrary pull Vince heaved himself over the side. Grounding his feet to stabilise the rowboat, he gestured to Hai to go drop the anchor. Li Hua ran to help. Taking the strain they held the small boat steady while Hai, having successfully anchored the larger vessel, freed the tow rope. Stumbling in the surging waves they hauled the rowboat onto the sand.

"You should have waited. You are not strong enough yet!" Li Hua chided. Vince raised his hands in mock surrender.

"I couldn't ... disappoint ... Hai ..." he gasped sinking down into the sand head between his knees.

It was a while before he could stand. Even then he needed help to stumble back to his temporary abode. Collapsed in bed, he listened helplessly as Hai received a tongue-lashing.

Li Hua turned. "And as for you, words fail me ..." but Vince was oblivious to the coming tirade, eyes closing he sank deeply into dreams ...

The boat was bobbing on endless water, stars spun above his head. A face materialised, a face no longer shattered, a face smiling with joy ...

"Jase, Jase ..." he mumbled, reaching out.

"Let it go Vince," the voice was familiar, though somehow softened. "It's OK, I'm fine, no more killing, no more revenge. I never wanted that ... This is your second chance, a second chance for the whole world. You know where hate leads, teach the children, teach them to let it go, to choose peace. They need you Vince. You were a good brother to me, always ..." The face dissolved, only echoes remaining, transforming, as Hai's face loomed.

"OK? Ge ge OK?" Hai questioned anxiously. Vince nodded.

"Hi! Hi!" He mumbled in his acquired Chinese. Impulsively he pulled Hai under his arm, ruffling his hair. Hai couldn't understand why Vince was crying, only that he was saying those magic words. "di di, di di, (little brother).

"Ge, ge," he pronounced wrapping his arms around Vince. Had he now earned his "big brother" status Vince wondered?

He slept well that night and successive nights. Hai was emphatic that he rest, forgoing even their daily trip to bathe in the stream. Instead he appeared with an old plastic bucket with which he hauled fresh water for Vince to wash in. Though they had few words to communicate, comradery was tight.

Li Hua appeared the second evening, a large bowl of rice and vegetables in her hands.

"To celebrate," she announced. "It's my mother's speciality."

"What are we celebrating?" Vince asked.

"Your recovery. Hai tells me you are better now. That you want to go to swim in the big pool." Hai looked apprehensive. Vince guessed he understood, "swim" and "go" being firmly ensconced in the boy's vocabulary. No word had been said of pools or swimming on Vince's part, but he chose not to expose him.

"Yes," he winked at Hai, who cracked conspiratorial a grin. "I'd like to, if it's not too far. I'm still getting over our last escapade."

"It's not far, but maybe wait one more day, to be sure. I'll go with you just in case. It's pretty deep in parts." Vince bit back a remark that he was a strong swimmer ...

"What about the rice harvest?"

"Finished."

"Will the others come back then, the other adults?" Her reply was long in coming, something was troubling her. He reached out, but she moved away. "Look lady, I'm not trying to hurt you. You just looked upset ... Is there something you're not telling me?"

"No, nothing! Just don't touch me, OK!" Scrambling up she headed off down the beach, eyes streaming. Hai, not understanding the preceding English, looked questioningly at Vince.

"Li Hua ...?" he made a face.

"Angry. Sad and angry." Vince made the requisite expressions. Hai glanced furtively at the retreating figure then began to draw in the sand, simple stick figures. He pointed to himself.

"Ge, ge." Did that mean he was the eldest?

Vince remembered John's message. On another patch he drew

figures with triangular skirts. "Boys, girls," Vince prompted, writing the words under each group. Hai nodded saying the words over. He then drew a large stick figure pointing at Vince.

"Man," Vince pronounced, again writing the word. He knew what was coming, a large skirted figure. "Li Hua?" Hai nodded. "Woman," he wrote as Hai repeated. Vince pointed to the small stick figures. "How many?" Hai didn't understand. Vince pointed to his fingers and began to count. Hai complied flourishing both hands ... 10 ... 20 ... 30 he paused for a moment to pull down some fingers with his thumb.

"32?" Vince confirmed it with his own fingers. A similar procedure established the girls. Vince was not surprised, he'd seen them. Now came the clincher. He pointed to the word beneath his stick figure.

"Man?" Hai raised one finger and pointed at Vince. "Woman?" A solitary finger emerged.

"Li Hua," Hai stated.

"Woman? Man?" Vince raised his hand to his eyebrow as if looking around. "Woman, man?" he asked again. Hai shook his head, eyes welling tears. He jerked his finger across his throat, the meaning all too clear. Vince hugged him.

"Di, di. Di di and Ge ge." He whispered. Hai nodded, fighting to contain the tears. "It's OK, it's OK."

Vince began to draw his own picture in the sand, a man and a boy.

"Ge ge. Hai." He announced pointing. Hai nodded. Making a large circle he drew many small stick figures some in skirts. He wrote the words "boys" and "girls" then added one large figure. "Li Hua?" Hai nodded ...

"I saw the children." Vince ventured over his bowl of rice. "I followed Hai this morning. Don't be angry with him, please. It's not his fault." Panic flickered in her eyes. Resisting the impulse to reach out to reassure her, he kept his hands imprisoned in his lap. "I won't hurt you or the children. I want to help ... God sent me to help you." He muttered, cringing at the unaccustomed words.

"God?" she questioned, panic easing a little.

"Yes, and my brother, the one who was killed." He looked for ridicule, there was none. "I dreamt he came to tell me to help you care for the children, to be their ge ge," he whispered, eyes clouding. How was it Chinese had separate definitions for brothers, words that could bring such strong emotions? "Please, let me do it for him, let me help them too. It's true I've seen fighting and killing, but I know where it leads. I can teach them not to be bitter and vengeful like I was." The tears were welling now, but his tears always softened her heart.

"If you stay you need to understand – you don't touch me!"

"OK. If that's what you want. You have my word I won't touch you. Look it wasn't like I was trying to get you in bed or something. It's like with Hai, when he's sad I give him a hug or ruffle his hair to tell him I'm there for him. It's not about sex."

"Don't tell me you don't want me. I've seen how you look at me, how all men look at me!"

"OK, I'm a man. I can't help that. Any man would be crazy not to want you. I can't help it if my eyes stray sometimes, but I promise my hands wont."

"They always do, men are liars!"

"Not all men. Surely you must have known some who treated you with respect." She hesitated.

"There was one ... but he's gone."

"Si wan?" She nodded, eyes clouding.

"Your husband?"

"No, we were not lovers. Si wan he was ... he ... he was like my big brother. He looked after me. He helped me when they took me, taught me how to bare it ..."

"Who took you? Government?" She nodded.

"Damn bastards!" Vince swore. "Damn them to hell!"

"Si wan said God killed them all, all the ones with the mark."

"Yes, they're all dead and gone now. I guess God's vengeance is better than mine."

"You were angry?" She looked up. God she was beautiful, if

106

only ... Vince restrained himself.

"Yes, I was angry. I wanted to take revenge for my brother, but I was wrong. It ate me up from the inside."

"You need to tell the boys, some of them are angry too. They've seen dreadful things, things a child should never witness. Maybe God did send you, perhaps you can get through to them. Each child has a story, even Hai. He escaped when they came to take his father. His brother helped him escape. They slid off the back of the boat, hid underwater. They heard the gunfire, saw their mother and sister hauled onto a boat. He never saw them again."

"So Hai has a brother?"

"Had a brother, a big brother ... He died later."

"I want to help them. Please, let me stay, let me help?"

"Will you swear you won't touch me. You said it was God who kept you across the ocean, who sent you here. Will you swear on His book? He'll take vengeance if you lie, like he did on the soldiers." She pointed to the Bible Vince had recovered from the boat. He placed his hand on it.

"I swear never to try to touch Li Hua again without her permission. I promise never to hurt her or any of the children."

"Why did you add that bit?" she questioned angrily. "I'll never give you permission, ever."

"Perhaps when you come to know and trust me, you'll let me take your hand when you're upset, or you can cry on my shoulder when you're sad." She was placated, though Vince knew in his heart it wasn't the real reason.

13

Next day was the beginning of a new life for Vince. Li Hua introduced him to the children. Most giggled and smiled, but some, he noticed, held back, a surly expression on their faces. One called out angrily. Li Hua said something in Chinese. The culprit scowled down at the floor. Vince had no time to ponder the matter, as he was seized by myriad tiny hands each vying for his attention. Hai yelled something, and they fell back, he seemed to have some authority with them. Choosing a girl, and boy from the little ones, he placed one on each of Vince's hands. The girl gave a cheeky grin and began to pull Vince toward the trees. The boy looked up timidly, a little awed at being chosen. Hand in hand they followed Li Hua down a well-trodden path.

"Where are we going?" Vince asked.

"To the pool of course!" Li Hua responded. Children crowded around them, sometimes prodding, or pulling at his shorts. Hai followed behind trying to keep them somewhat in line.

The pool was deep and shaded, the water refreshing. The children swam well, he noticed even the smallest. There was much splashing and horse play among the older boys, even so he noticed how mindful they often were for the little ones. Were there other ge ges here or were they all "brothers"? It seemed not. He noticed certain groups hung together. The boy who'd been admonished sulked slightly apart from the throng, throwing him occasional angry glances.

He wanted to ask about him, about what he'd said, but was too caught up in the melee to seek out Li Hua. These kids had no father, had expectations that he might play with them, hold their hands, ride them on his shoulders. His strength was soon exhausted. Li Hua drove them away with harsh words and flapping arms. Gratefully he reclined on the bank to watch the fun. She joined him.

"I'm sorry, they are too excited to listen. I should have known better than to bring them here with you." Li Hua apologised.

"It's OK. I've had worse believe me. I just wish I was strong enough to handle them all, but I'm still a bit of a weakling."

"You'll get strong again and they'll get used to you being around."

"That boy, the one who's so angry with me, what did he say?"

"He thinks you are government because you look like the guy who burnt his village."

"I do?"

"All westerners look the same to us at first, especially to a child. I told him you're not government, that you fought against the bad soldiers, but he doesn't believe me."

Vince looked at his reflection in the mirror. Beard gone, his bare chin was several shades lighter than his face. The sun would soon take care of that. He'd wanted to get Li Hua to cut his hair too, but reflecting on the angry glances, he decided it might be better to get away from his usual military image. He pulled a comb through the mess of sandy curls, annoyed at their stubborn rebellion. Li Hua's smile appeared in the mirror behind him.

"So, the razor worked OK?"

"Well enough. I might search around for something better, it's too damn hot for a beard." She stood considering him. It makes you blend in more. Chinese men don't grow beards, at least not thick ones like yours."

"With my colouring I'm never going to blend in much."

She smiled. "That's why you're so interesting to them."

"And why some of them hate me."

"That can't be helped. They'll learn eventually. Perhaps you should take a Chinese name?"

"Such as?"

"I don't know, let me think about it. For sure most can't say 'Vince' can they?" She laughed. His attempts to teach his name to the youngsters had proved futile. Hai referred to him as ge ge but clearly this title could not be assumed with most of them, many had or had had big brothers whose place it would be futile to try to fill.

An eager voice chirped up beside them. Vince waited, catching the tone of the sing song conversation.

"Hai has found the perfect name!" Li Hua pronounced. Vince frowned, not sure what the mischievous Hai might have in mind. "Bohai!"

"It sounds like Hai's name. What does it mean?"

"It means elder brother sea. You are his new elder brother brought from the sea. It's perfect!" Vince smiled and ruffled

Hai's hair.

"Yes, he's right. It is perfect."

Days took on a relaxed rhythm. With Hai as his constant companion, plus a frequent crowd of observing youngsters, he explored the nearby area. The children having returned to the beach dwellings, Vince spent the cooler part of his days checking and reinforcing the lean-tos, afraid some of the flimsier ones might collapse on their occupants should a storm come, but then storms never seemed to come anymore. Long-term he wanted to build huts, to fix the rudder of the boat, but that would need to wait on a trip to the city to scrounge for the necessary tools etc.

During the hot part of the day, he slept or indulged in language exchanges with Hai. His Chinese was coming on at last, complicated by the realisation that many spoke a different dialect and switched freely between the two. He tuned in to the constant chatter of children always keen to teach him a word or two. He got to know some of them, though their names mostly eluded him.

Hai was disgruntled at having to stay behind. Li Hua had been insistent that she needed him to help the girls watch over the little ones. She'd called him "the most responsible" and hinted that should anything happen, the girls would need a "man" around. Pleasing as these things might be, he didn't relish babysitting while she and Bohai went to the old city to look for tools. Bohai was his ge ge, he should have been allowed to go along. He was old enough! He sat, chin in hands, gazing sullenly at the sea, all but ignoring the throng of children he was meant to help supervise ...

It was a couple of miles walk to Hualien. Vince had hoped to use the time to glean more of Li Hua's story, but she was not forthcoming. He switched to easier topics, learning some of the history of the city. People came from the west coast after World War 2, she explained, eager for land. There had been many stories of ghosts, ploughed up bones and skeletons. The area had been a battle ground as US troops sought to evict the entrenched Japanese, many bodies were never recovered. It was long ago, but she'd never felt comfortable about the stories. Now there were more dead, more "ghosts" to inhabit the ruins ...

"That's why I took the children away, it's better by the sea. I only come here to look for things we need. I don't let the children come, who knows what they may see."

"Bodies?" Vince queried.

"Mostly just bones now, they don't last long in the tropics, but the place is still full of rats and scavengers." Vince nodded remembering another city.

The smell was different here, a heady mixture of age and decay rather than the putrid smell of decaying flesh. Perhaps it was due to the passing of time. Vegetation had sprung up everywhere already masking many of the remains of the simple homes and habitations. They began their search. It wasn't easy. When they finally located the garage Li Hua recalled from former years, it was nothing but an overgrown, blackened shell.

"Looks like the gas tanks went up." Vince stated. "Did you have the earthquakes here?" She nodded.

"Hualien has always had earthquakes, but none like that. There were mountains there before. She waved toward the surrounding hills. The mountains where my people lived ..."

"How did you? ..."

"We, Si wan and I, we were down in the city, even then we were lucky to be alive."

"What about the children? Where they in the city too?" She shook her head, tears welling.

"Only a few, like Hai. We went to look, to search for our villages, but there was nothing left, only the children. They talked about lights that came out of nowhere, that snatched them up, spirits maybe ..."

"I saw them too ... I ... I was ..." She looked up expectantly. Vince changed the subject, not ready to reveal anything further. "Were they all together, the children?"

"No, we found them in twos and threes, some all alone."

"They must have been scared stiff. How did they survive?"

"No, they were calm. They were expecting us to come ..." her voice trailed off. There was a noise behind them. Vince spun round but could see nothing.

"Probably one of those scavengers you were talking about."

She shuddered. "Come on, let's keep looking, I don't like this place, too many ghosts." Vince opened his mouth, then closed it abruptly. Easterners were a lot more superstitious he was discovering. Besides, who was he to say these things didn't exist. He'd seen Chad, and Jace, maybe ...? He longed to take her hand to reassure her but resisted the urge.

"Yes, you're right, let's keep looking." There was the noise again! Compulsively she grabbed his arm. He looked down at the fingers, then at the fear filled eyes.

"Stay here, I'll check it out."

"No, don't leave me Vince, please ..."

"I'll only be a moment, probably a stray dog or something." For sure it wasn't a rat. He gently released her fingers, sorry to end so quickly this first intimacy.

Creeping forward, he listened intently. It was coming from the balcony of a half-demolished, flat roofed, bungalow. Warily he entered. Perhaps it was a stray, maybe something more sinister. Perhaps there were more children ...? Ascending the stairs, he was alerted by a small grating sound. Leaping clear, he barely evaded an avalanche of corrugated iron and debris. He heard Li Hua scream. Scrambling over the rubble he ran up the remaining stairs. A door swung feebly on its hinges but there was no sign of an assailant. Li Hua was yelling his name, again and again.

"I'm OK!" he yelled, mounting the balcony.

"Come back ... please, come back ..." She was sobbing, frantic with fear.

"I'm coming." He took a quick look around before proceeding but could find no clue as to the identity of his attacker. Perhaps it was an accident? He thought not.

Li Hua was shaking. She clung to him hiding her face in his

chest.

"They've come back!" she sobbed. "Don't let them get me again! Please don't let them get me."

"Don't worry, I'll keep you safe, you and the kids. It's OK." He stroked her hair endeavouring to calm her. Instantly she pulled back. Vince released her immediately spreading his arms in a consolidatory fashion. She looked confused. The embrace had been comforting, but she knew better than to trust a man.

"I'm just trying to help," Vince muttered frustratedly. "Look if you really can't trust me maybe it's better I go, but whatever it was that caused that fall, it wasn't friendly ..." She looked remorseful.

"I'm sorry Vince ... it's just ... If you only knew you'd understand ..."

"How can I know if you won't talk about it?"

"I will, but not now. I just want to get out of here."

"OK, but what about the tools? If we don't get them now, we'll have to come back. You can go if you want, I can find my own way."

"No, I don't want to be alone. I'm ... I'm afraid of the spirits."

"They can't hurt you, they're dead and gone. The only 'spirits' I've seen, if you want to call them that, were the good kind. The men who hurt you are gone forever and I'm here to protect you now, you and the children." She nodded.

"Come with me then. There must be something I can use around here."

"There ... there was a workshop under the main offices ... I didn't want to go there ..."

"OK, just show me where it is, you don't have to come in."

"It's down this way I think."

Vince heard a scuffling sound echoing their footsteps but couldn't leave Li Hua. He could come another time to investigate.

It was not far to the shell that had once been the municipal buildings, housing the military elite. Li Hua began to tremble. He held out his hand, as to a frightened animal. Hesitantly she took it.

"Don't worry Li Hua, you're safe with me." The words echoed within, "You're safe with me." He'd told Candy the same. He wished he had a rifle. Someone or something was following them. "God, or whoever you are, keep us safe," he whispered under his breath. He'd always had hate to drive out the fear, but now with Li Hua beside him and a bunch of children reliant on them he felt vulnerable. Perhaps they should have just turned back?

"The workshops, they were underground. There was this ramp they drove down, through the parking area."

"OK. Let's look around, maybe we can find the entrance."

"There. It was over there, by the sign."

Delving among the debris Vince shook his head. No way they'd get in that way.

"Were there stairs, a lift maybe?" She nodded. He led her up the steps, dodging piles of concrete and glass. The main doors were gone, as was much of the framework, the wall black, embedded with scars, but if it had stood this long it was unlikely to fall now. Vince proceeded cautiously, Li Hua lagging behind. The lift shaft was nothing but an empty hole. Pushing aside the debris he discovered the stairs. Li Hua looked anxious. He didn't want to risk leaving her, but he'd feel better with some kind of weapon in his hand, a wrench maybe. He eased himself through the gap wishing he had a flashlight.

"Come on Li Hua. Take my hand." Gingerly she edged forward clinging in the darkness as their eyes adjusted to the half-light.

"It's too dark." She whimpered, "please, let's go back. I'm scared."

"OK, OK, It's alright. I'll take you back. I can come on my own another time and check it out. I'll need some kind of light anyway." He liked the way she clung to his arm, fear overcoming her distrust. Soon they were out of the building. He took note of its location. If she were right, there must be a treasure trove of tools and supplies down there.

There were no noises on their way back and soon she released his arm. He said nothing, knowing something had changed between them. Though there were no more "intimacies", and she once more kept her distance, a barrier had been removed. She was starting to trust him. For his part he remained on guard, aware any further contact must remain in her court.

As a boy he'd once befriended a racoon. He'd found it behind a skip, foraging for food, a misplaced rodent, an inner-city dweller like him. There'd been a strange affinity between them. He'd left it food every day, gradually growing closer, and closer, till finally it would come eat from his hand, allow him to pet it even. There'd been a savage pleasure in the secret alliance, boy and rodent, both alone, unloved, finding solace in each other. He never discovered what happened to it, just one day it was no longer there, didn't come to his call. Probably rounded up and sent back to its natural abode, or more likely killed.

Li Hua, while far superior to the raccoon, reminded him of the creature, pretty and harmless looking, but fierce and wild if you got too close. He'd bide his time. Li Hua was worth waiting for. Besides what other choice did he have?

"I don't want you to go Vince! There are ghosts, spirits, back there. Please, we don't need the tools that much. It's dangerous." She grabbed his hand, eyes imploring. They'd been over this the night before on their return.

"Look lady, I think you're right. There is something or someone back there, but I don't think it's anything to do with ghosts. They might want us to think that, but the only spirits I've seen were helping us."

"But you don't understand, those men were evil! You wouldn't believe the things they did." Oh he believed her all right. He'd been one of them. She'd not told him her story as promised. He'd not thought it the right time, it would only cause her to be more upset. Whatever it was, it could wait. He didn't like the idea of someone, something, lurking there in the ruins. Suppose it followed them back to the children ...

"Look Li Hua, I have to go. Not only for the tools. Whatever that was, and for sure it was something, I need to make sure it doesn't come here and hurt one of the kids." That silenced her.

"You'll be careful!"

"I'll be careful. Don't worry, I've done a lot of this stuff, believe me. I couldn't bare for anything to hurt any of you." He let go of her hand, gently stroking her hair, intimacy to intimacy. She did not pull away.

"I come Bohai!" a shrill voice called, bare feet running across the sand towards him.

"No Hai!" He'd expected this. Hugging the scrawny form under his arm, he ruffled his hair. "Hai stay here, stay with Li Hua. Li Hua needs a ge ge."

"Bohai need Hai! One no good, two good! Ghosts fight Bohai. Hai strong. Hai help!"

"No Hai." Vince crouched so their eyes were level. "Vince better alone."

"Alone?" Vince struggled to find words Hai would understand. "Hai strong, Hai here with Li Hua." The boy shook his head rebelliously. Hai could be stubborn. "Hai here!" Vince said strongly. Tears welled in the boy's eyes. Finally, with a look of defiance he stormed off. He was angry, Vince knew the feeling. He'd felt the same when his father had gone and never returned ...

It was for his own good he told himself as he trudged on toward the city, looking back every now and then to make sure Hai hadn't decided to follow him, as he'd followed his father. He remembered the alley, the muffled groan, the blood ... He set it aside, such things were long gone, at least he hoped they were. What lay in the ruins he didn't know, but he was determined to find out. First, he wanted to check the basement. He'd feel better with some kind of weapon in his hands.

There were no noises this time, only an occasional rustle among the debris. He found the place easily enough. After a brief reconnoitre, he turned on his old flashlight, replenished with batteries from Li Hua, and squeezed past the blockage on the staircase. Below he found all he could wish for and more, stacked neatly in order like some ancient museum to a past age.

He worked swiftly, selecting the best and most versatile. He gazed longingly at the welding torch with its accompanying gas cylinder, exactly what was needed for the rudder, but how could he haul it back up the stairs or all the way to the beach? He could bring the rudder here, but he had a bad feeling about this place. Shouldering the pack, now heavy and cumbersome, he set off back up the stairs. A loud crashing preceded him. Heart pounding, he flickered the torch over the cloud of dust and debris blocking the exit. There was no mistake this time, someone was trying to kill him.

The lift shaft! Perhaps he might climb out through there? The doors had been smashed by the impact of the falling car which now lay diagonally across the entrance. Crawling gingerly over the base he was relieved to find it didn't shift. A quick exploration with the flashlight however revealed smooth metal sidings and the cables and lifting gear coiled around the top of the smashed vehicle. No way to climb. His only hope lay in Li Hua, would she dare come looking for him?

Time passed with agonising slowness. Saving the torch battery, he slumped in the dim light of the lift shaft. She will come, she will come, he told himself, but when? How long would it take for her to overcome her fears. He recalled her terror. Superstition was rife in these third world lands. Certainly she and Hai believed in spirits. Did he? Was some unseen force of retribution seeking to punish him? There'd been the kick of the pony, the fire, the bullet that missed him and killed Candy and his child, the broken rudder. Again, and again he'd cheated death, but was death pursuing him still?

"You gave me a chance! I want that chance." He yelled into the darkness. "I want to live and help rebuild." A noise rang out above, a voice shrill with fright. He knew that voice. Hai. It was Hai. He must have followed ...

"Hai! It's me Vince! – Bohai! it's Bo Hai! Don't be scared. I'm down here in the lift shaft."

"Bo ... Bohai? It you?" The voice was clearer now at the top on the shaft.

"Yes, it's me. I'm OK. Get a rope." Vince cursed the darkness. Rope was not a word Hai knew. "Get Li Hua. Li Hua come." Hai reeled off something in Chinese, Vince didn't recognise the words. He heard shuffling above. Why was he not going for help?

"Get Li Hua!" he repeated again, and again. There was a splintering sound above. Why was he not going? Was Hai in danger? "Hai! Hai! Can you hear me?" No answer. Something was coming down the chute, clanging dully against the metal siding. He squinted his eyes trying to pierce the shadows but could see nothing. He moved back warily, risking the torch. It all became clear – a firehose nozzle! Hai was resourceful, but would it take his weight? There was only one way to find out. Gathering the slack, he wound the hose around his arm testing his weight. It seemed sound enough. The only other choice was to wait while Hai went to get Li Hua or scavenge something else. It could take hours, meanwhile whoever did this might be up there with Hai. He decided to risk it. Coiling it around his body he used his legs to help push up the wall finally emerging to a pale, but triumphant, Hai reaching to help him over the rim.

"Hai! Hai!" Vince grabbed him, hugging him tight, ruffling his hair.

"Bo Hai not mad?"

"No, not mad. Hai good boy. Smart boy!" Vince tapped his forehead. Hai's look of trepidation turned to a grin, then sobered.

"We go, no good here!"

Vince nodded, with a sigh for the pack of tools still lying in the basement. It was enough for one day and besides he didn't like having Hai here, whoever or whatever could still be around.

Li Hua met them along the way, running, teary eyed to embrace them both in turn. Vince noted the hug.

"I was so worried. I thought ... I didn't know what happened to you, you were gone so long. Then I realised Hai was missing ..." She glared at Hai yelling a bunch of Chinese at him. Vince set a protective arm around the boy.

"Don't get mad at Hai, he saved my life – well maybe. Certainly, if not for him, I'd still be trapped in the cellar."

"The spirits? You mustn't go there again! None of us should "

"I didn't get the tools. There are plenty down there, good quality too, but I didn't know how much weight the hose would take."

"Hose?" Hai began chattering in Chinese evidently recounting his part of the episode.

"He said he thought you were a ghost, that you were yelling something, and your voice was coming up through the floor. He was really scared."

"I bet he was. I would have been too, but Hai is a very brave boy, smart too, thinking of the fire hose." Hai grinned as she recounted what he'd said ...

"You said you'd tell me ..." They were alone on the beach. Behind them the children were settling down to sleep. Even Hai, exhausted after his adventure, had relinquished his usual evening perch at their side.

"OK." She was tracing patterns in the sand, avoiding his eyes. He waited.

"Our home was high up in the mountains, we thought we were safe, that no one knew about us. Then soldiers came out of nowhere and surrounded the village, helicopters with guns and jeeps, to take us to camps ... or so I heard. I never got there. As they were loading us onto trucks this soldier grabbed my arm, I couldn't understand what he was saying. My father tried to stop them, but they just hit him with their rifles. They kept on hitting him. I never saw him again nor my mother or brothers ..." She stopped for a moment seeking control.

"You don't have to tell me if it's too much ... I know what they do ..." He remembered the woman they'd found in the camp. She'd been insane. Li Hua, it seemed, had survived her ordeal.

"Si wan, he saved me."

"He rescued you?"

"No one could rescue me, or my family, but he helped me survive ... Si wan was famous. Everyone knew of Si wan. Many thought he betrayed his people, but it wasn't like that. He did what he did to try to save us. He'd send food and medicine, tried to warn of the raids. When we were taken, he would try to help us."

"So, he was a soldier of some kind, an agent?" She looked puzzled at Vince's conjecture.

"No, no, he was a dancer, with the most wonderful voice. It's one of the traditions among our people, young men dress as women and dance. It's something like your drag queens, but different – tradition. My people are famous for this, but it is only to entertain. Our men are renowned for their beauty. Si wan, he was very beautiful, very skilled, no one could tell he was a man. At first they hired him to play jokes on their guests. He thought perhaps he might endear them to his people, protect us, but then it changed ... he told me ... but we are not telling his story but mine ..."

"Go on."

"There were other women. They told me what to expect, even so that first night ..." She stopped, eyes wild, breath catching.

"They raped you." She nodded.

"Again, and again. There were three of them, all officers. They used me like an animal." Her eyes glared in fear and anger.

"You said Si wan saved you?"

"Yes," she was breathing deeply. "He told them I was a dancer ..."

"Were you? A dancer I mean?"

"All my people dance. He had me dance with him for the commandant. He taught me things, how to entice him. He said I had to find a protector. The man was a beast, jealous and demanding, but he kept the others away. Si wan taught me how to go to a secret place in my mind, a place they couldn't touch me ..."

"That's all over now, all over. No one can hurt you now, I won't let them, not you, not the children." She laid her head on his shoulder. He remembered the racoon, resisting the temptation to draw her into his arms. He must let her make the first moves. Damn those men for what they'd done to her. It wasn't like it had been with Candy, Candy had been a worldly woman, even revelled in her role, Li Hua had been an innocent.

She went on, whispering against his chest, to tell of the purges, how her people were decimated, how, at great risk, she and Si wan sent food and supplies to those still holding out hidden in the secret places of the mountains. It had all been for nothing her people had been destroyed, all but these children.

"Are they all from the villages?"

She raised her head. "Not all, some, like Hai, are Han Chinese, but they are all my children." Her eyes flamed protectively.

"They are becoming mine too, even though I'm a "wai guo ren". She half smiled at his reference to being "a foreign devil".

"You are a good man Vince." He smiled. It was not an epitaph used for him before, for Chad, for Rat, but never him. Some day he should tell her his own story, but not now. Perhaps not ever. He basked in the warmth of her approval ...

"Don't go! Please, don't go Vince. We need you!"

"I have to go and find out who or what it is lurking there, before it hurts one of you. You have to understand that."

"Then I'm going with you. Two are better than one."

"If anything happened who would take care of the children? Can't you see I have to go alone."

"Hai won't let you, he'll come after you like last time."

"Not if he doesn't know, and he won't if you don't tell him. I'll leave early before the sun comes up. He's a heavy sleeper Hai." She grabbed his arm, resting her head against it.

"I'm scared Vince."

"I know. That's why I have to go take care of it ..."

The movement awoke him instantly. Leaping up, he grabbed the metal bar he now kept in reach. Startled eyes met his own. He replaced the rod.

"What are you doing Li Hua?" The eyes faltered, in the moon-light.

"You go risk your life tomorrow. You do it for us, so tonight I sleep with you. We ..." Vince held her at arm's length.

"No Li Hua."

"You want me. I know you do." Her hand slid enticingly down his chest.

"Yes, but not like this. You are not a commodity to be given as a reward or something."

"What is 'commodity'?"

"A thing you can buy or sell, give or retain. I don't want you to think about me that way."

"How do you want me to think about you?"

"Like a woman should think of a man, as her protector, with or without sex. I want you, but only when you want me too, not once but for always."

"Like a wife?" Her voice was strangled.

"Yes, like a wife, a wife who enjoys her man touching her." He stroked her face. Caught off guard, she shrank back instinctively. "See? You are not ready yet Li Hua. Now go. Please go! I'm no saint and I can only stand so much of this."

She turned, flustered. No man had ever refused her before. Did he mean it? Did he want to be like a husband to her? Would she want that? She was coming to trust him, but the thought of having to share a man's bed every night made her feel sick, the more so because she wasn't sure it would work with him to go to that secret place. This was different, too personal ...

14

Vince set off through the darkness. He'd slept little, his mind going over and over last night. Had he been wrong? Had he just blown the only chance he'd have with her? He felt himself a good lover, certainly Candy considered him so, he knew how to please a woman. But those women had been willing, or easily won over by a little foreplay, Li Hua was different. He didn't want her going off in that "secret place" she'd told of, enduring his touch out of duty. He wanted sex with her, sure he wanted sex, but was that all? He wanted a companion, someone to talk with, to just chill with when all the children were asleep. Hai was great, but communication was limited. Only she spoke his language, only she could understand. He wasn't prepared to gamble that away for a mere night's revelry. He'd known what it was to be alone out there in the ocean, day after day, just him and the sky, even the stars far, far off and out of reach. No, like Racoon he'd accept the relationship on her terms, whatever they might be, even if it meant living the rest of his life in celibacy. He recalled Candy, her warm, sensual body pressed enticingly to his. He felt his blood rise. Frustrated, he punched into one of the palms skinning his knuckles.

"Fool!" He muttered to himself.

The trip went surprisingly smoothly, there were no noises, no falling debris, or indeed anything out of the ordinary. Whatever or whoever it was appeared to have gone. Vince retrieved the tools via the lift shaft without problem, using the ropes he'd brought for the purpose.

He returned to find an angry Hai.

"You go! Hai no come!" the youngster yelled. The usual hug and hair ruffling were repulsed. Li Hua came to his rescue, unleashing a stream of Chinese that sent Hai running off rubbing his eyes.

"Tell him why I couldn't take him," Vince pleaded.

"I did, repeatedly. Just leave him, he'll calm down in a while. You got the tools I see. She nodded at the bulging backpack ... Any trouble?" She was trying to be off hand but the catch in her voice gave her away. Vince pretended not to notice.

"No, nothing at all, everything seemed quiet. Maybe they moved on. I thought it best to bring the tools back first."

"First? You mean you're going back?"

"Not today, but yes, I have to be sure it's safe. Who knows what might be lurking around there."

"It's the ghosts, Vince. I told you."

"Whatever it is I intend to find out. I was thinking, they've attacked me twice, but never you or Hai. Is that a co-incidence? Why me?"

"Perhaps ... perhaps it's the commandant ... maybe he ..."

"It's not Li Hua. He's gone, gone forever."

"But you don't know how he was ..."

"I think I do."

Vince arranged the tools neatly against the wall. He had a mind to fix the rudder first. Hai desperately wanted to sail the boat. It might help him get over his hurt at not going along. He thought longingly of the workshop, of the welding torch and metal sheeting, but he was not easy with staying down there any length of time till he was sure it was safe. Instead he set to work on a tree he had preselected. He was unfamiliar with the species, but the wood seemed good and hard.

The children came to watch, till Li Hua shooed them away, wary of the hatchet. Hai was nowhere to be seen. It was a slow process making anything from wood without the requisite power tools, but as impatience subsided, he found the pounding of the waves leant a natural rhythm to the work. For thousands of years men had worked wood, building boats, houses, ploughs, whatever was needed. There was a strange fulfilment in it, of continuation. Sweat coated his back as the sun grew stronger, it was nearing midday and his exertion and early rise were catching up on him. Gathering the tools, he returned to the shelter of his hut. He should find a more secure place to keep them, he reflected, a place safe from curious little fingers. Not all these kids were angels.

A noise outside awoke him. Voices were raised, Hai's angry, commanding. Shaking off his sleepiness he went to look – nothing. He resumed his work bringing the panel into the shade of the lean to. He wanted to release what was left of the tiller. It would be easier to fit the wood to that than to try to make a new one, but it was probably a two-man job – he needed Hai. He could at least take a look. Perhaps if Hai saw him making for the ship, he'd come along.

It was not the case, and, while Vince could easily free the rod that once held the rudder, he'd need someone in the water to catch it. It was not so deep there, but the bottom was craggy and full of weed. It would be difficult to find once lost. Sighing he swung back into the rowboat and headed ashore. The wind was picking up and clouds beaded the horizon, perhaps they were in for rain?

From nowhere, a shot rang out. It missed Vince by miles. Whoever was shooting was no marksman, or perhaps it was the rising wind that deflected it. He was taking no chances. Someone was out to kill him. Dropping the oars, he slipped into the water kicking for shore, using the boat as a shield between him and the trees from which the shot came. There was no further shooting. Li Hua came running. The shore filled with children who she tried to shoo away. So many faces, but not the one he looked for, Hai was not there. He remembered the raised voices by his hut. Had Hia been kidnapped ... or worse?

"Hai? Where's Hai?" he asked desperately as he stumbled ashore tethering the rowboat.

"Hai? How should I know! Vince, someone was shooting at you! For Christ's sake will you believe me! It's the commandant, he said he'd kill any man who touched me ..." She broke down in tears, crumpling on the beach to sit rocking, arms encircling her head. Children milled around, confused.

"Go, go!" Vince yelled gesturing. One of the older girls said something in Chinese which seemed to work, and one by one they retreated to the huts. He bent to comfort Li Hua, but she pushed him away.

"Go away Vince, don't come near me, he'll kill you, I tell you!"

"It's not him, Li Hua! And even if it was, I'd fight him for you, ghost or not. He's never going to touch you again, I swear it!" Ignoring her protests, he engulfed her in his arms, holding her tight to his chest till she stopped struggling and sobbed into his shoulder. She looked up, eyes swimming.

"You can't stop him Vince, you can't fight a ghost, no one can ..." She began to pull away, but he held firm. A thought coming to him.

"Listen Li Hua, it wasn't the commandant, it wasn't a soldier of any kind."

"You don't know that."

"Yes, I do. The shot was way off, even allowing for the wind, it missed me by miles. If it had been him it would at least have hit close by, winged me or something. Now listen, do you know where Hai is, I'm worried about him?"

"You look Hai? Hai no want Bo Hai!" A form emerged from the trees, from the direction of the shot, striding off sulkily to join the others. Vince stood staring, mind racing ... surely not, not Hai? Hai had been in the building looking for him, the most likely place for a firearm ...

Again, Hai did not join them at supper, sitting off on his own at the far edge of the group of children.

"He'll come around ... eventually." Li Hua noted with a smile. "Hai can be stubborn sometimes. It's not only you, I've seen him quarrelling with some of the other boys too. He's just sulking."

"I hope so. Only ..." She looked up.

"Only?"

"Nothing important," he lied. He would not put his apprehension into words. Hai wouldn't do such a thing over a silly childish tiff, but then how well did he know Hai really? These kids had been through so much who was to say they hadn't been affected in some way ...

That night his dreams were disturbed. He awoke, restless, to pace the beach. Moonlight glinted on the surf as the waves broke over his feet, sucking away the anguish in their peaceful withdrawal. It was not a fear of death or injury, they had been his constant companions for years, it was a fear of betrayal, of perfidy. Hai had filled his brother's place, but had he been mistaken? Perhaps, perhaps not. He made a decision. If it should turn out to be Hai, he'd forgive him. Life and love were too precious. He'd found mercy, a second chance, he owed it to Hai to extend that to him. Perhaps it wasn't Hai at all, perhaps it was a co-incidence, certainly it seemed unlikely Hai had caused the first two incidents. Why had he rescued him if so? No, it must be someone else ... but why had Hai been coming from that very spot? Perhaps the incidents were unrelated? Perhaps his attacker had given Hai the gun, but why would they do that ...

He slept late. The sun was well risen when Li Hua appeared.

"Not like you to sleep late. You haven't even touched your breakfast." He glanced at the bowl. She answered the unspoken question. "Hai didn't bring it, he's gone off somewhere. I sent one of the girls with it." Vince picked it up.

"Do you know where he went? He should stay with the others till we find out who fired that shot."

"Try telling that to Hai. He was gone when I woke up. Do you need help? With the rudder I mean ... I could ask one of the other boys?"

"Let me go look for him first, he can't have gone far. We were to do it together ... I ..."

"You don't want him to feel bad."

"Yes. There's no rush about the boat, I was doing it mostly for Hai."

"Be careful. It seems it's you they're after. Maybe I should go look for him."

"No, stay with the kids, there's work to be done and I know nothing of farming here." She was reluctant to let him go, but if Hai was involved, he wanted to face him alone, in secret.

Vince scoured the surrounding area. No sign of Hai. The sun was hot, he should return to camp. Reluctant to quit he gave one final check of the area the shot came from. Rat would have checked for tracks ...

There they were, there'd been no attempt to hide them, boy's footprints around Hai's size. Most of the children went barefoot, but they were younger, smaller ... It must have been Hai ... he struggled to believe it. The old hardness kicked in. He'd been a fool, should have known better than to let people in ... Angry, he returned to camp. Again, no sign of Hai. He rummaged through Hai's sleeping place, disturbing the other boys, looking for clues

... or the gun. Nothing.

"Vince, what's wrong. Why are you so angry? You're scaring me." Her voice was shaky, eyes wild. He must stop, get control. Racoon, remember the God damned racoon ... Breathing deeply he calmed his exterior.

"It's Hai," he spat out. "I saw him coming out of the trees down where the shot came from ..."

"No Vince, you're wrong!" she interjected. "Hai would never ... You don't know him like I do."

"I just saw the footprints. Who else has feet his size around here? There's a place he hid out, the undergrowth is all crushed and broken ..."

"No, I don't believe you, there must be some explanation."

"Come, I'll show you." He grabbed her arm dragging her toward the trees. She pulled away angrily.

"Don't touch me!"

"Sorry, I forgot." Cursing his anger, he sought to regain control. She hesitated, then followed.

"See? This is where he hid, and here are the footprints ..." He turned.

Suddenly Hai was there, eyes wild.

"Go! Bohai go!" This was not the sulky boy, there was fear in his eyes. "Go!"

"No Hai, we talk." Vince gestured to Li Hua.

"Go!" Hai began screaming in Chinese.

"Vince!" Li Hua yelled, but it was too late. Hai hurled himself at Vince as a shot rang out from the trees above. They hit the ground in a tumble of limbs and undergrowth! The tree shook as a boy leapt down and took to his heels, scampering off through the vegetation. Vince sprang to give chase. It was then he saw the blood, Hai's blood!

"No! no!" he yelled, the shooter forgotten in a spasm of guilt and grief. Li Hua was there instantly, pulling away the bloodied T shirt to reveal a mess of blood and flesh.

"I told you it wasn't Hai!" she hissed. "He was trying to save you!" Vince sank, head in his hands. He'd messed up every-thing! Training kicked in. Ripping a strip from his shirt, he used it to bind the rest in a wad to stem the blood flow. He knew it was useless, an emergency unit might have saved him, but there was no such unit now. He could put Hai through the agony of taking out the bullet minus anaesthesia, but he'd die anyway. Tears of futility coursed down his cheeks. He hadn't been able to save Jace, or Chad, or Candy and now Hai! Worse, he'd thought Hai had betrayed him. Guilt flooded his soul, even as he bound the wound, even as he carried him in his arms back to camp. His body functioned independently, as it had with Candy, as it had with Chad.

"How bad is it?" Li Hua peered anxiously at the pale face, the flickering eyes. He didn't need to say anything, she could see. He laid him gently on his bed.

"Should we try to take out the bullet?" she asked. Vince shook his head.

"No point. Let him go ... in peace ..." Their eyes were stream-ing, Vince's voice breaking.

"You loved him." She seemed surprised.

"Of course I loved him! That's why I was so angry. Better for him I never came ... better ..."

"It wasn't your fault. He should have told us about Jiao-long."

"Jiao-long?"

"It's too late now ..." The eyes flickered open.

"Ge ge, OK?" The voice was weak but audible. He lapsed into Chinese.

"He says Jiao-long made him swear he wouldn't tell about the gun. Some of the other boys were in on it too, but they didn't want to kill you, just make you go away. They stopped Jiao-long many times. Hai pretended to be mad at you so they'd trust him. He thought if he told you, you'd go away ..." Her voice trailed off for a moment. "He lost his brother because he was afraid. Now it's OK, he saved you ..." she began to sob uncontrollably. Vince cradled Hai's head in his lap. He didn't have words to say what he wanted, and Li Hua was past translating. He knew the guilt, the torrent of emotion, for he too had been a coward. He confessed it, finally. He could have saved Jase, had he used the automatic ... had he not hesitated those few vital seconds.

"De, de ... Bohai love Hai ... Hai brave ... Hai strong ... Hai save ge ge ... The words were little enough but a smile traced the blue tinged lips.

Hai lingered into the evening, his lucid moments becoming increasing rare. They had nothing to give him for the pain. Vince could bare it no longer. Excusing himself, he stumbled out of the hut. Confronted by a sea of small, worried faces, he shook his head. The boy who fired the gun was nowhere to be seen. Jiao-long she'd called him. Later he'd hunt him down ... and then what ... retribution on a child? He couldn't think straight, his heart, so recently softened, was torn in pieces. Striding down the beach he found no comfort in the waves, in their eternal rhythms, the pain was too roar. Out of earshot of the children he collapsed to his knees.

"Why?" He murmured, "Why? Why is it always like this?" His voice grew at every word till he was yelling, screaming at that eternal presence which had preserved him so many times. "Why not me? Why did they die? Why did they all die? Why is it me still here! Take me instead, not Hai, not Hai ... please ..." His voice ebbed into sobs. Face engulfed in hands and knees, he didn't notice its coming. Not till light invaded his senses did he look up, cringing at the sight. The orb spun exuding the brilliance of the being within. Again, Vince was overwhelmed by the awesome power emanating from the presence.

"You have questions. The answers are not yours to know. You would not comprehend." The voice was soft, cajoling, like a father with a small child too ignorant to grasp things far above it. For all that, the passion still burnt in his heart.

"You healed me once. Heal him. Take me instead, God knows I am not fit to live, but Hai he ..."

"God knows it. He knows Hai also. You cannot make deals with Him. Yet this child is needed, he has a role to play here before coming home."

"Home, is that what you call it?"

"You are angry because you don't understand. There is a plan, just as there was a plan to bring you here. All you have been through is part of that design, part of your healing."

"I don't want healing. I want Hai to live!"

"He is part of your healing and so much more you cannot foresee. He will be a great blessing to his people."

"You mean he'll live. You're going to heal him?"

"Yes, I was waiting only for your intercession. Hai needs healing too, healing for many things, you all do. It will come slowly, bit by bit, day by day. You are part of that healing, part of the plan ..."

"What about Candy? What about the child?"

"You will have others, you and Li Hua. Candy's healing needed to be accomplished elsewhere. It would not happen here. As for your child, it will never know the things you have suffered. She shall know only joy."

"Then they live on?"

"They do. You have sought and found redemption, but there is a plan for the whole earth, for every being. You cannot take in the vastness and complexity of the plan. Do not try to comprehend, know only that God loves you, you and Hai and Li Hua and Candy too. He even loved Brady, though she is beyond his help for the present."

"Then you will heal Hai?"

"He is already healed. It is part of the plan. Come, let us go together. He may be scared, you must tell him I am coming, not to be afraid."

Vince ran down the beach, the sphere of light pulsing above.

"Don't be scared! Don't be scared!" he yelled as the children ran screaming. "He's come to heal Hai!" but they didn't understand.

Li Hua looked up alarmed as the hut was engulfed by light. Vince plunged through the door.

"It's OK. He's come to heal Hai. You're going to live Hai, you're gonna live!"

131

Hai's eyes flickered open, confused. Vince was there holding his hand, telling him not be afraid. A feeling of warmth swept through his body, tingling, strengthening. He held tight to Vince as wave after wave swept through him, the pain receding and joy unbounded filling his heart. Li Hua sat mesmerised, breathing in the echoes of light as they dissipated around her.

Then it was gone. Hai sat up smiling, sound, unmarked, save for a small round scar. A remembrance of the place that death had entered. He began rattling off in Chinese.

"He says you brought the angels again," Li Hua translated, breathless. Hai's arms opened. Vince engulfed him in a tearful embrace. Then Li Hua was there too, arms wrapped around them both. Small faces peered timidly around the entrance.

"Lai, lai," Li Hua called, reverting to Chinese. The message was clear even to Vince.

"There's been no sign of him," Li Hua said as she handed Vince the rice bowl. All around faces guzzled, breakfast bowls close to mouths, chopsticks flying.

"I'll go look for him."

"I don't think that's wise. He still has the gun. Let me go look."

"No, Hai go," Hai garbled, his mouth full. He wiped his lips with the back of his hand as he set down the bowl.

"No, Hai! I can't risk losing you again!"

"Jiao-long, Hai. OK." He lapsed into Chinese. Vince awaited the translation.

"He says he thinks he knows where Jiao-long is hiding, that he won't hurt him. He meant to shoot you, not him. He has a point."

"I don't want him to go, who knows what will happen?"

"Hai's been there before when he tried to shoot you ... at the beach, remember. You need to let him go."

"Then I go with him."

"No, you'll only put him in danger. Let Hai and I go." A heated discussion began in Chinese. After a few minutes Li Hua explained. "He doesn't want me to go either, says Jiao-long will run away if he sees me coming. You said Hai was healed because there is a plan for him. He will help his people, fulfil his destiny. Don't you see, that means he won't be hurt. You owe it to him to trust him, we both do." Vince was reluctant but finally yielded to logic. The conversation continued. "He wants to know what will happen to Jiao-long if he comes back. Will he be punished?"

Vince's anger flared for a moment then reduced to a steady heat.

"He needs to learn his lesson ..."

"Don't you think he's already learnt it? He and Hai were friends before you came. He must have seen what happened. Can you imagine how he must feel? He's just a boy." She had a point. Vince could imagine the pain of killing a friend. He thought of Chad, of Rat. How would he have felt?

"OK, OK, you win, but I intend to keep a sharp eye on him in future and he has to give Hai the gun before he's allowed back."

Li Hua translated. Hai scrambled to his feet, eager to commence his quest. "Take care!" Vince called after him. There was no need to translate.

Jiao-long cowered in the half-ruined shack. Once, long, long, ago his grandfather had lived there farming the surrounding paddy fields. Now the fields were gone, it was all gone, overgrown, but the shack, such as it was, had survived. His stomach cramped with hunger. He dared not go out, his only venture had ended in disaster. The boys had seen him, thrown stones and angry words. Hai was dying they'd said. "Xiongshou! Xiongshou!" they'd called him – murderer! Had they gone to get the wai guo ren? Were they even now seeking him? He'd thrown the gun away. He had no means of defence if they came. Would they torture him as they had his father ...? He must hide, but where better than here? Only he and Hai knew of this place and Hai was dead ... he'd killed him ... He recalled the nightmare image as he scrambled from the tree, the blood. He'd thought it was the enemy's blood, but it wasn't, it had been Hai's. It was all the foreigner's fault. Li Hua had said they were all dead, but it wasn't true. Why hadn't they just left him there on the boat to die, why did they have to save him? It was all a façade his trying to be friendly. He wasn't like them, could never be like them, even if he did take a Chinese name, even if he shaved off the beard. He'd fooled Hai and now Hai was dead. Hai was dead and he, Jiao-long, had killed him. The anger fended off the guilt and shame ...

There was a noise outside, someone was pushing through the concealing undergrowth! Why had he thrown away the gun? He grabbed the wooden post with its nails protruding, raising it defensively above his shoulder. They wouldn't take him easy. He'd fight to the last as his brother had done ...

He took a deep breath as the door creaked open, sunlight flooding in. The stick fell from his hand. He yelled, covering his face and eyes from the awful apparition.

"Bu! Li! Li!" He screamed, imploring the figure to leave him alone, but it ignored him. Moving closer it spoke rapidly, denying its ghost hood, jabbering nonsense, that Bohai had called a spirit to come and heal him. He cowered, scared, his bravado leaving him ...

"We should go find him," Vince argued. "He's been gone too long!"

"We must trust him," Li Hua replied portraying a calm she was far from feeling. "I don't suppose it will be easy to persuade Jiao-long to come back. Anyway, we don't know where he went." She was right. Why hadn't they established a time?

Vince became increasingly restless as the evening came on. Beside them sat two bowls of rice reserved, unclaimed, as supper came and went.

"We have to go look," Vince urged. "Perhaps he wasn't strong enough yet. We should never have let him go!"

"He'll come back Vince. He's not Jase. You can't live in fear of it happening again."

"It almost did ..."

"But it didn't. They intervened and will again if needed. We have to learn to trust."

"Easy for you to say!"

She looked down. "No, actually it's hard, harder than you know ..." The racoon ...

"I'm sorry. I'm a stupid, self-centred dolt."

"Not entirely." She smiled. "If I can learn to trust you, then you must learn to trust Hai. We must all trust each other, it's the only way to leave the past behind." She looked away. Vince gently turned her chin to face him.

"And do you trust me, Li Hua?"

"I'm starting to ..."

They were interrupted by a commotion among the children. Li Hua jumped to her feet. A scuffle had begun. Her calls ignored Vince moved quickly to break it up. A number of boys were involved, plus a particularly vindictive girl who emerged from the scrummage, a ragged piece of shirt in hand. The combatants melted away before Vince's onslaught leaving two figures jumbled on the ground. It was Hai! Thank God it was Hai. He knew before the face emerged who was the other – Jiao-long. Voices erupted in high pitched clamour. Vince waited impatiently for the translation.

"Why was Hai fighting him?" Vince demanded.

"He wasn't." Li Hua threw over her shoulder. "He was trying to defend him from the others."

It was a while before the full story emerged, how he'd taken Hai for a ghost. How, true to Li Hua's surmise, it had taken a long time to convince him to return and how he'd then been set upon by the children.

Jiao-long was surprisingly surly, nursing his bruises and a rapidly blackening eye. Another racoon to coax, Vince surmised. Li Hua took the boy in hand. Rejecting her motherly comfort, he seized eagerly on the rice bowl. Would he have done differently at that age? He thought not. LI Hua had told him some of Jiao-long's history. It had been hard enough for Vince to see his father stabbed, Jace blown to pieces, but at least it had been quick. By all accounts Jiao-long's father's death had been anything but. They'd wanted information and they'd got it ... in the end. No one knew why they'd let Jiao-long go, perhaps to spread the word of what would happen to those who opposed the regime. They'd been wrong, Jiao-long had spread only hate and anger. It would have been easier to forgive if it had been him he shot, not Hai, Vince thought, but that was unfair. The bullet had been meant for him in revenge for his father. He understood that ...

15

Night passed. The sun rose to greet a new day, new, but permeated by the tattered rags of yesterday. Hai was not in his usual place, curled up like a puppy in the corner of Vince's shed. Instead he was sleeping with Jiao-long, guarding him from the insults that flew when Li Hua was not around to stop it. Forgiveness was hard for these kids and he had hurt one of their own. Vince wondered what would have happened if it had been him. Would they have reacted the same? He suspected not. A bond had been forged between the children and Jiao-long had broken that bond, albeit accidentally. Hai had said there'd been other attempts on his life, that other boys had helped stop. He must talk with them somehow, explain. Li Hua would translate, but what would he say? The truth! He must tell the truth, how he had been like them ...

He rose to walk the beach. It was early, the sun a mere glow over the sea, leaving the "West" behind, enlightening this new west, this new horizon. He too must leave the darkness behind and embrace the sun. It wasn't easy, and it wasn't a one-off thing, he had to keep moving forward and this was the next step. Would his words drive them away, drive Hai and Li Hua away? He desperately wanted to stay, to be a part of this new beginning ...

Vince drew in a deep breath. This was the hardest thing he'd ever done. The younger children had been taken off by two of the older girls. Curious eyes regarded him. Jiao-long sat to one side, Hai his only companion. Would he find himself likewise rejected if they knew? Courage wavered. Should he stop before it was too late? No. The only way to be free was to tell them, otherwise all he built would be on a false foundation, built on a lie ... Li Hua looked over expectantly. The children were growing restless.

"I wanted to tell you my story. We all have stories, why we act as we do, why Jiao-long did what he did ..." He listened as the translation echoed his words. "I was once like you. My father died when I was ten ... I ... I saw it ..." He hadn't expected the emotional torrent that came with the confession. Small eyes empathised. They understood ... "He ... he'd started getting angry, so angry. There was never enough money. I know now he took drugs ... the drugs did it. My mother couldn't handle it. She left, taking my little brother with her. She would have taken me, but I wouldn't leave my father. I felt she was deserting him. Then, one night, he was worse than usual. He said he was going out ... He wouldn't let me go with him. I knew something was wrong, so I sneaked after him. He went down a dark alley ... I was scared, hung back. I heard this muffled sound, a gurgling noise. I ran into the alley and there were these two men leaning over something on the ground. They ran off when they saw me, and I went to look, it was my father. I yelled and yelled for help but by the time someone came he was dead ..." Vince struggled for a moment to regain his composure. He felt an arm around him as Li Hua pulled him to her shoulder. It was comforting ... No, he must go on with the story ...

"I went to live with my mother after that, but it was hard. She wasn't very smart and didn't earn enough to keep us all. I was angry and defiant, blaming everyone for what happened to my father. Inside I blamed myself. If only I hadn't hung back, if I hadn't been a coward ... As soon as I was old enough, I joined the armed forces. I wanted to earn money any way I knew how. More than that, I wanted to exact revenge for the hurt I'd suffered." The eyes changed, some hostile. Li Hua was adding something.

"What did you say?" he whispered.

"I explained this was many years ago, before the world government." He nodded, continuing.

"Like Li Hua said, this was long before the World Government took over. At first it was OK. I kept myself to myself mostly. Training was intense, and it helped ease the anger and the pain. Back then we were fighting covert ops against the newly formed 'World Government' ..." Li Hua hesitated.

"What are covert ops?"

"Secret missions. The US went the diplomacy route, but the military ... well you know how that goes." Evidently she did, for the translation continued amid whisperings. He noticed tears on Jiao-long's face.

"What's with Jiao-long?" he hissed.

"His father was a resistance fighter ..." Understanding dawned ... He paused before continuing. The truth, the whole truth! He reminded himself.

"Then ... Then they dropped the nukes. The entire eastern seaboard was destroyed including the seat of government. They just walked in during the ensuing chaos and took over everything. We had a choice, co-operate or die. Some guys refused. They were shot ... I was not one of them." Jiao-long's tears were replaced by an angry glare. He yelled something, and Li Hua yelled back. Chaos ensued. After a few minutes a stubborn silence was regained.

"What did you say?" Vince whispered.

"That they must listen to the end before they judge. I told them you were supporting your family, that you had to protect them. It's true, isn't it?" Vince nodded.

"Yes, it's true." That had been part of the reason, but not all of it.

"Before the nukes, I could see their side. They wanted to destroy the power of the big corporations, bring justice for the poor and ..." Li Hua waved for him to stop. She was a while explaining it seemed. Finally, she signalled for him to continue.

"My dad was smart, he had his own business, but he gct screwed over – (cheated)" he added, seeing Li Hua's confusion. "– by the big money guys. It was after that he started on the drugs. I was wrong, the new government were just as bad, even worse, but like Li Hua said, I had my mother and brother to think about. The worse things got, the more Jase began to rebel I ... I told him to just go along with it, to pretend, but he wouldn't listen. Our assignments got worse and worse. At first it was 'rebel forces', split offs of the armed forces, or self-styled vigilantes, but then it began to be civilians, demonstrators. I got to where I didn't care, my heart was hard as nails. There was so much anger in me. Jase, my brother, he tried to talk to me. Asked me to go with him to join one of the rebel armies, but I wouldn't. I didn't care if I got killed, but not Jase, not my brother. I hoped my being in the forces would protect him and my mum, but it didn't ..."

"I was there when he was killed. It was at one of those secret meetings the government had infiltrated. I tried to stop them ... I ... I hesitated just like I did with my dad ... I might have saved him if I'd acted sooner ... There were only two of us on the stairs ... I ..." He realised Li Hua had stopped translating. Someone was squeezing his hand. It was Hai.

"Finish it Vince, you have to finish it," Li Hua whispered. He nodded trying to pull the shreds of control together.

"After that ... after that, me and some other guys took off with a bunch of stuff, guns, equipment and so on. We went way up in the wilderness. At first it was just to escape, some had families ..." Hai said something. Li Hua translated.

"He asked if you took your mother?"

"No, she died. She died even before all that happened with Jase." He continued. "There were other folks who escaped, living out in the wild, peaceful types mostly. We tried to protect them, setting ambushes for the government troops when we could." Hai spoke again, eyes gleaming.

"He says you were like Jiao-long's father then."

"No, I can't claim that, not really, Chad and Rat and some of the other guys, that was their motivation. With me it was the anger. I wanted revenge, revenge for Jase, revenge for my own life ..." Li Hua did not translate immediately, he suspected she was adapting it in some way.

"I want them to know, Li Hua, to understand what all that hate made me into. I ..."

"So they will, in time, but enough for today. Sometimes the truth must come in small doses. They've been through so much, but they are still children. Healing comes a little at a time."

A myriad of small voices bled into the silence.

"They want to know how you got here?" Li Hua was right ... Skipping the Brady episode, he related only that he had been escaping bad men when the rudder had broken. Remembering Hai's recent healing he added that God had kept him across the ocean and brought him to help them, thus ending on a more positive note.

"That must have been hard," Li Hua whispered squeezing his hand before endeavouring to calm the melee caused by his tale. Emotions flared within.

"I need some time alone Li Hua," he said rising to his feet. She nodded, calling Hai who'd risen to follow. A space cleared before him as he strode off down the beach, faces confused, questioning, fearful? He relished the sound of the waves, the relentless ocean surging over his feet and ankles. He delved deeper into the flow, allowing the water to lift him from his feet. Like the waves, his past was being washed away, surging and withdrawing. He looked up toward the rocks that had sheltered him, imprisoning his small craft like the fingers of God. He began to swim. It was not far, still he felt the strain of weakened muscles as he sought a place to clamber up.

Sitting aloft he gazed out over the ocean, losing himself once more in its vastness. He felt light, even a little giddy. Was it the exertion of the swim or perhaps the admissions of the past? As one who has vomited, he felt both better, yet somehow weak and vulnerable. He had put into their hands the means to hurt, to destroy him. He'd let down his defences, allowing these children and most of all Li Hua into the secret vaults of his heart. He didn't care, anything was better than the hate and the pain. Somehow, he knew he'd been accepted, forgiven, by a force beyond his understanding, a force of love and compassion, a force that brought him across the ocean and set him here in this rocky haven. Somehow that was enough. He yelled out over the waves, his voice mixing with the sound of the wind and the sea birds. Tears, not of sorrow, but of joy, coursed down his face. Salty breezes brushed his lips, refreshing waves licked at his toes. He sat, at one with his surroundings. He was at peace ...

It came to him slowly at first, just an inkling, a warm shadow within the heart. He wanted to be loved. Not the passionate coupling he'd had with Candy, more than the tight comradery of Chad and Rat, more even than the protective bond between him and his brother. He'd sought it in his father, his dysfunctional mother. All had disappointed, none had filled the empty vacuum, the raw wounds he carried within. When it came down to it people were a mess, each with their own scars and handicaps, even Li Hua, even Hai ... Only one love was perfect, never giving up, never taking the easy path of complacency ... He could see it now, his journey to redemption, littered with rocks and stones, joy and pain, the sweet and the bitter. He knew now someone loved him more than Jace, more even than Chad, who had intervened for him. Someone who, like Hai, was willing to give their life for him, so he could walk free of the hate and anger that had so long clouded his vision, a divine presence, deep as the ocean, relentless as the waves, washing, washing away the past, the hate, the pain ... He knew it was an ongoing process, that he must give as he'd been given. He must forgive Jiao-long, again, and again if necessary, till he too could be freed. Gazing at the endless infinity of sky and sea, he felt his own insignificance, a tiny cog in an infinite wheel, yet loved, unconditionally, infinitely. He bathed in the presence of God.

The sky was darkening, the sun sliding behind the trees, gilding the shoreline, as a wet hand shook him awake.

"Li Hua!"

"I came to see if you were OK. I figured you needed time alone, but when you didn't come back, I thought maybe the swim out here was too much for you. I can get Hai to bring the rowboat if need be." He smiled, motherly Li Hua, always caring, nurturing.

"No, I'm OK. I was just taking all this in and must have nodded off." He gestured to the ocean.

"I'd have thought you'd had enough of that on your voyage."

"I had enough of being alone, yes, but never enough of this ..."

"Yes, I know what you mean." She set her head against his shoulder. "That's one reason I chose this place. We all have need of healing ... I ... I talked with the children. They understand, even Jiao-long... I think he wants to make peace. He made an idol of his father, but when he saw how they finally broke him, how he gave away the others ..."

"He realised he was only human, like the rest of us ..."

"No. it wasn't that way. He couldn't accept it, he felt he must be more than his father to expunge the guilt. Then when he couldn't ..."

"I understand. I forgive him. I was angry because of Hai. I deserve to die, but Hai ... Hai was innocent."

"No one is truly innocent. Hai ran away when they took his brother, he still has nightmares about it sometimes. That's why he did what he did ..."

"Hai is a great kid. They all are. We'll help them get over it all, you'll see." He put his arm around her shoulders hugging her to him. She looked up and without thinking he kissed her. It was only a light kiss, nothing of passion. She didn't resist but drew off after a moment. Vince raised his arm.

"I'm sorry, Li Hua. I just forgot ... You know I care about you, you and Hai and it just seemed so natural ..." She smiled.

"It's OK, I know. I can feel the difference when you touch me. It's not like the others. Maybe ...?"

"Not till you're ready." He kissed her forehead, easing her back onto his shoulder. "I was thinking, perhaps we should get married ..." She looked alarmed. "Don't worry," he added, gently tapping her nose. "It doesn't mean you have to have sex with me. I just thought … I love you Li Hua, and I want to prove it to you. If we never have sex, I'll still love you. That's not why I want to marry you. I want to belong to someone … I …"

"Yes!" Vince was startled at this sudden admission. "Yes, I'll marry you Vince. I need someone too … and … if you give me time. I promise it wont always be like this. I'll heal, just as we are all healing."

"I can wait." He bent over to kiss her forehead again, but she tilted her head to catch his lips, shy, hesitant, like a virgin with her first kiss. She blushed, embarrassed. Tactfully he said nothing, cradling her head once more on his shoulder. It felt good there.

"We don't have a priest or anything?" she ventured.

"Don't need one. We'll make our promises to each other. God will hear. Who needs a priest when angels come visiting?" He nuzzled her ear playfully. "The children would like it. It would be like a new beginning for them too." She giggled, nodding.

"OK, enough of this Vince. I need to head back. I left the girls to serve the evening meal and those boys have big appetites. Can you swim back, or shall I send Hai with the boat?"

"We can swim together."

The sea echoed the harmony of their strokes. They were evenly matched, Vince's strength slowly recovering, but not yet sufficient to out do her. They emerged laughing to find Hai standing at the water's edge, rattling off in Chinese.

"He says he kept food for us," Li Hua translated, "and … Jiao-long wants to say something." She raised an eyebrow. They could see him alone on the edge of the crowd. He approached looking as if he wished the earth would open and swallow him. He stopped before them, eyes set to the sand, mouth sullen and rebellious.

"I sorry." he mumbled.

"It's OK," Vince opened his arms. Jiao-long resisted, but he hugged him anyway. "How do you say forgive?" he hissed to Li Hua.

"Yuan liang."

"Bohai one leeang." Vince struggled with the unfamiliar words wanting to reciprocate Jiao-long's effort. Giggles surfaced from Li Hua. Soon even Jiao-long was laughing at Vince's ineptitude. Hai said something.

"What?"

"He says maybe we all have to learn English," Li Hua translated between gasps of laughter. Grabbing Hai, Vince tussled his hair in their own version of affection. Jiao-long looked on, both envious and critical of their bond. Enough for today, Vince thought, remembering the racoon. They had time, lots of time ...

16

"So, tell me, what was so funny about my Chinese?" Vince asked between mouthfuls.

"Well ..." she smiled. "Maybe I should teach you. There are tones in Chinese – like singing, and you need to learn pronunciation and maybe some grammar."

"You mean I did it all wrong and made a fool of myself?"

"I wouldn't say that. He understood, that's the important thing. I think it was good, it made it easier, more relaxed."

"At my expense!" He grinned. "I don't think I'm a natural with language."

"Don't worry, I'll help you. We'll have more time together if we're to share a hut."

"You want to? Share a hut I mean?" She flushed.

"Just to sleep."

"I know, I know." He raised her hand to his lips, kissing the palm. "I want you to know you can trust me."

"I do, Vince, I do trust you. I just need a little time." Hai looked up, curious what this sudden intimacy might mean. Li Hua said something. His face lit up and he ran off yelling something to the children.

"You told him?"

"Yes, I thought he should be the first to know."

"Definitely, but what about Hai? He always sleeps in my hut."
"Don't worry, I'll talk to him, explain. He'll be fine."

Hai wasn't fine, even Vince could see that. He'd hoped they could finally fix the rudder on the boat, but Hai seemed to have other ideas. Was he avoiding him? Li Hua had gone to tend the rice fields, and without her translation it would be hard to find out what was wrong. He'd seemed so happy about him and Li Hua getting together last night. Could it be about the sleeping, maybe Hai didn't know how it was with married people? He'd seen some of the boys making obscene gestures this morning. It had annoyed him, but he felt to interfere would only make things worse. Perhaps they'd been talking with Hai? Finally, seeing Hai sitting alone eating, he grabbed the opportunity. Hai turned away, bowl on his bottom lip, shoving rice into his mouth. Vince pivoted, removing the bowl with a slight struggle. The eyes were tearful.

"Hai sad. Why?" He added the necessary gestures. Hai glared angrily.

"Bohai, Hai's ge ge. Li Hua say Hai no sleep ge ge . Li Hua sleep Bohai." Ah so that was it. Vince thought for a moment.

"Hai big, strong, like man. Man no sleep with mother. Hai need own room." Hai looked puzzled.

"One room?" He questioned. Vince drew a rectangle in the sand and set a dividing line in the centre.

"Bohia and Li Hua sleep here. Hai big boy. Hai no sleep with girl. Hai's room." He pointed.

"Bohai man. Bohai sleep Li Hua?" Hai retorted. This wasn't going to be easy.

"Bohai and Li Hua marry," He slid an imaginary ring on his finger.

"Boy say ..." Hai coloured. "Boy say Bohai Li Hua make ..." finding no word he crossed his arms in a cradling motion.

"Baby." Vince clarified replicating the motion. "Yes, Bohai and Li Hua make baby. Hai big boy, not look Bohai make baby."

"Bo Hai make baby, Hai go out." Hai looked jubilant, thinking he'd found a solution. Vince sighed.

"Not easy make baby, many times to make baby, maybe baby, maybe no baby." How much of this Hai grasped he didn't know. "Hai big boy. Big boy have own room. Hai help, make hut for Hai, Bohai and Li Hua, big hut. We make it." He pointed to each of them. Hai looked hesitant.

Looking down he mumbled, "Bo hai, Hai's ge ge?"

"Yes, Hai, Bohai's de de." Vince scrambled for words, Hai's English was far better than his Chinese, but it was still a struggle to explain. He pointed to his heart. "Bohia's heart – big hole." He scooped sand to make a hole gesturing back and forth. "Hai here," pointing to his heart. "But hole very big, Bohai love Li Hua, love boys, love girls, even love Jiao-long. Hole very big. Hole hurt Bohai." He gestured repeatedly to his heart. "Bo Hai need lots to fill heart, but Hai first, Hai here first." A smile was slowly spreading across Hai's face.

"Hai and Bohai make hut? Hai help ge ge. Hai big boy, not sleep girl?" Vince nodded clasping him to him. The boat would have to wait a while longer.

"It seems Hai is expecting a little sister in the near future," Li Hua confronted Vince over supper.

"Look, I'm sorry. He was upset, I was trying to explain, and one thing led to another."

"It's OK," she smiled. "Let him think that for the moment if it helps, just remember I can't have children. Even if things work out between us there will be no baby."

"Who knows, after Hai's healing anything can happen, but like I said, I'm not marrying you for sex or for babies, I just want to be with you. He dropped a kiss on her forehead. There was sniggering behind them. "Maybe you should talk to those boys," he whispered. "From what I've seen they don't have a very good attitude towards women."

"Can you blame them with all they've seen? I'll talk to them, but I don't think it will do much good. It would come better from a man."

"Yes, I know, another reason to work on my Chinese, meanwhile I intend to set them a good example of how a married couple should be. They'll grow up one day, and the only girls around are their friends' sisters, imagine how that will go if they don't shape up."

"Seems we have a big job ahead of us."

"A job I'm happy to undertake. Now, did Hai tell you about building a hut?"

"Of course. He talked of nothing else. I think he wanted me to know it was a man thing, just you two. We can wait while you build it."

"You won't change your mind, will you?"

"No, but I have a notion to try to find a dress or something. A woman shouldn't get married in shorts and a T shirt. It would make it more special to dress up ... for the children I mean." Vince chuckled, under her efficient exterior her femininity was slowly emerging.

"Why not? You have time while we build the hut. Maybe you can find something for me while you are at it. What do Chinese men wear at weddings?"

"Nowadays they wear suits, but perhaps we should start something new – trust me?"

"I suspect I'll regret it, but yes, I trust you Li Hua. Just don't make me look too ridiculous."

He and Hai began work the next day, drawing plans in the sand, pacing out a good position. Hai was a little put out that Vince insisted on Li Hua's input at this stage.

"Tell him, after this the rest will be a surprise, but as we all will live here, we must all help decide. Tell him a good man thinks about what will make his wife comfy, what will be practical for her." Hai seemed mollified and Li Hua winked.

"Maybe tomorrow could you come to Hualien with me?" she asked as they headed off to get the tools. "I know it's safe now, but I'm still scared of the ghosts."

"Sure!" Vince and Hai exchanged glances. Vince got the message.

Work went well once the initial problems were overcome. The palms, with their straight, tapering trunks locking together at the corners, needed little of the gouging and trimming required in that long-ago pine cabin Rat had taught them to build. Besides there was no real winter here, no need of the plugging or tight fit. That was just as well, he was no engineer. The main problem was the hauling. The older boys had quickly got the vision and come to help, but even choosing only the younger, lighter trees, it was hard work.

The sun shone between the slats dappling the inner ground. They'd decided on three rooms inside at Li Hua's suggestion, a main room where they could be together and two bedrooms leading off. It was more work, but he could see the sense of it for Hai's sake. Even Jiao-long had joined in the work, the sullen scowl slipping into a grin as the day went on.

By evening they were tired, but jubilant. Vince's back and shoulders ached. The girls, he noticed, kept on the edge of things bringing food and water, caring for the younger ones under Li Hua's supervision. Roles seemed more clearly delineated here. He pondered if women had enjoyed the freedom of their western counterparts even prior to the one world government – he suspected not.

"You've done well!" Li Hua, finished with her serving, passed a bowl. "Do you still want to come to Hualien with me tomorrow or would you rather carry on with the work here? The boys seem to be enjoying helping."

"Tell the truth I'd be glad to take a break. My back is killing me. Don't tell the boys though."

"Don't worry I won't tarnish your image. I should think they need a break too."

"Well, if they don't now, they will in the morning. I used to be able to do all this kind of stuff no problem. That transpacific sail knocked the strength out of me."

"I'm glad of it. I'd have been too scared to come near you otherwise. This way as you get stronger, I can trust you more.

Would you like me to massage your shoulders, or would that give the game away?" Vince thought for a minute.

"Well, if I'm to be the only male role model around here. I guess it's good they see my weakness, that I need your help too."

She smiled and set down her bowl. "No, finish your food first. You're to be my wife, not my servant." She looked surprised.

"Look, I don't know how it was before. I mean ... I know all you've seen of men is abuse, but what was it like in your family, before the soldiers and all that?"

"My father was a good man. He didn't beat my mother. He loved her."

"Did some of your men do that?" She looked at the ground.

"Sometimes ... Chinese men, they do it too ..."

"Where I grew up only cowards and bullies hit women. It happened sometimes there too, but there were laws against it."

"But the westerners, they were just as bad, worse sometimes ..."

"However it was then, we have the chance to start again, teach these boys right. Let's decide, no beating women, no beating anyone, and women should be free and equal, man and wife working alongside each other in whatever way works best. If a woman wants to cook and clean for a man, to bare his children, it should be from choice, from love."

"I love you Vince." Her eyes were moist with tears and he couldn't resist a kiss. The boys tittered, and Hai looked uncomfortable. He didn't care, they'd have to learn, and this was part of it.

Li Hua seemed to know where she was going, he thought, as they scrambled through the wreckage which had once been Hualien.

"It's around here somewhere."

"What exactly are we looking for?" he ventured, "a dress shop?"

She smiled. "No, a tailor. I saw one here before, but I had no reason to investigate then."

"You're hoping they'll have a wedding dress?"

She smiled. "Not exactly. My people loved bright colours, beads, embroidery."

"I hope you're not expecting me to wear something like that?" His head filled with pictures of exotic Polynesian women, but what in God's name did the men wear?

"Don't worry, no feathers, I promise!" she laughed. There was another side emerging from beneath her hard exterior, a shy girlish side.

The entrance, when they found it, was small, half hidden. Beyond a tiny office lay shelves of fabric, brilliant colours coated in dust and decay. Several sewing machines lay upended, on tables full of plaster and debris, mourning their lack of electricity. Li Hua seemed excited, loading the basket she'd brought with beads and trims, cottons and needles and casting an eye over the grubby reams of cloth.

"What about these?" Vince asked, crouching to inspect a pile of half-finished garments and hangers crushed beneath the remnants of a shattered metal clothes rail. Li Hua joined him, seizing on the garments with the joy of a child at Christmas. He left her to it. Strolling down the length of the shelves he had an idea. The outer surface of the cloth was dirty and soiled but further exploration revealed the inner layers to be untouched. Brilliant reds and purples flashed in dazzling silks and brocades. Bright colours, she'd said. He'd make a trip back with Hai, or maybe one of the girls ...

"I'll be outside," he called. Enough was enough! He recalled his mother's shopping trips, how he and Jase tried to avoid them. Jase was the more successful, Vince being the main beast of burden. The memories were less painful now, odd how they resurfaced ...

It was a while before she emerged loaded down with a bundle of cloth in addition to the overloaded basket.

"Here I'll take that." She looked surprised.

"If you take the basket, I'll take this. The basket is heavier."

"I'll take both."

"But you said your back hurt?"

"It's much better this morning. Didn't your men carry for you?"

"Sometimes, but we should share the load. I took a lot of things because I wasn't sure what would work."

"That's OK. Here, give them to me. You take that box sticking out if you want. I'm afraid it might fall." Reluctantly she passed the things.

"I don't want the children to think I'm lazy, that I make you do all the work."

"You, lazy?!" Vince laughed.

A commotion sounded as they neared the beach, childish voices and peels of laughter. Hai rushed to greet them, shouting.

"He says they have a surprise for us, a big surprise."

A host of small bodies parted as Jiao-long emerged in the centre, perched on the back of a huge cow-like beast, bare feet and legs kicking its neck to coax it forward. It raised large docile eyes as if to see what all the fuss was about.

"It's Jiao-long's" Li Hua interpreted from the hub bub. "It was his grandfather's ... It's a water buffalo. We use them to plough and pull things," she added, noting Vince's confusion. She continued in Chinese, then began to laugh. "I asked why he didn't bring it before, and he said he was afraid we might eat it!"

"Tell him the messengers said not to eat the animals." She looked puzzled but obliged.

Work proceeded quickly with the beast's help. Jiao-long gloried in his role. Large slanting horns aside, the beast seemed most domesticated, calmly ignoring the small bodies that frequently endeavoured to join Jiao-long on his perch.

Vince's secret visit to the tailor's shop went unobserved, and the girls seemed only too eager to help, giggling, and frequently arguing, about the best fabrics. Palm leaves had been spread over the roof beams and, although a little rough and ready, he was pleased with their work. He wanted to build more so all the children would have more permanent abodes.

All was ready, but Li Hua had requested one more day. He sat apart, pencil and pad in hand trying to decide exactly what his vows would entail. What should he say? There was the old wedding ceremony he'd been party to a few times, but he wanted something new, something becoming to this new life, this new Vince ... Crumpled pages sucked damp from the pool at his feet. Nothing came ...

"Wake up!" Hai shook Vince roughly by the shoulder. "Li Hua, girls, make – look, look!" Vince opened sleepy eyes taking in a flash of red from the bundle under Hai's arm. Red?? Just what had he let himself in for?

"OK, OK, Hai. I'm getting up." Pacified, Hai laid the clothes on the sheet beside him.

"See, OK?" Hai mimed trying on the attire. Hesitant, Vince eyed the neatly folded garments. On top lay a deep blue brocade figured with patterned gold dragons, interspersed with panels of red satin to form some kind of long waistcoat. Beneath he was relieved to see a simple pair of loose black trousers, drawstring gathered at the waist. Definitely not his style! Hai's brilliant smile drooped as he saw Vince's scowl. Picking them up he thrust them at Vince.

"Li Hua make for Bohai. Girls ..." he mimed sewing. "No make girls sad." He shook them at Vince glaring angrily. There was no way out. Vince hauled on the pants adjusting the waist. They were a little short, but maybe that's how they wore them. Hai helped slip on the waistcoat which he had to admit was a good fit if a little uncomfortable. It was a while since he'd bothered with a shirt. Hai looked him up and down braking into a smile.

"Beautiful!" he announced, having heard Vince use the word before. It didn't help, no use trying to explain ... Still, it was very eastern, whether Chinese or native Vince wasn't sure, but seeing Hai's face he realised he would have to acquiesce. It would please the children and most of all it would please Li Hua ...

Breakfast was served as usual. Vince, back in his shorts,

watched as Li Hua and the girls busied themselves around the pots and plates. He knew they were preparing something special. He and Hai had work to do also, moving their respective things into the new "house", smuggling in the reams of cloth under bedsheets etc. Some of the girls, in on the secret, looked over shyly. Gazing around Vince admired their creation. Bright coloured cloth hung from varied sections of the interior, sunlight, slanting through the slats, bringing to life the varied tones and patterns. Across the door swung a brilliant length of bright red silk patterned with exotic birds. The girls had insisted vehemently on the red, why, he wasn't sure. To his mind red conjured districts of ill repute, hardly appropriate in the circumstances ...

Work completed, he ventured outside. There was time remaining, Li Hua was busy with the food. He assumed, rightly, it would take her a while to get ready. He decided on a leisurely bathe in the stream, messing around and splashing with Hai and some of the other boys who joined them. Jiao-long was absent, spending much of his time in company with his old bovine friend.

Vince waited apprehensively for Li Hua to appear. Though bizarre and outlandish to his taste, the children seemed impressed with his costume. He wondered how he looked. He had only his small shaving mirror which proved useless. He knew his face, the sandy curls that now reached the waistcoat brim at the back, the fine creases at the eyes and dark tan that contrasted western eyes. He could never look Chinese, but maybe that was just as well. They needed to see not all westerners were evil. He had been once, but he understood he was here to represent Chad and Rat, John and the others, wherever they were ... It was not a lie, they were good men, and he ... he'd do his best to be like them, adding compassion to his courage and strength, and love... yes love, that stranger to his life. Would he find it here? Had he not already found it in Li Hua, in Hai, in the children ... Engrossed in thought he didn't notice as Li Hua emerged.

Even drenched in sweat in a dirty T shirt Li Hua was beautiful, but now ... He gasped in astonishment. A gold figured crimson robe contrasted flowers and ebony hair clouding loose to her waist. Chains and beads augmented the belt and vivid head-band, but all the finery could not eclipse the natural beauty of Li Hua.

"You like?" She swirled teasingly, settling the red silk rippling, a girlish pout adorning her lips. Vince was secretly glad of the loose trousers. He could see exactly what had held her captors enthralled. Stifling his emotions, he responded in part.

"I like, I like very much. You are so beautiful!"

"I hope you don't mind too much about your costume. The girls were set on it. At least I talked them out of the red. The blue is better, it wouldn't have suited you."

"Seems to me you didn't win all the way." He exhibited the red panels. "What is it with you guys and red anyway?"

"Red is for good luck. We always wear red for weddings." He remembered the vehemence about the door hanging. That ex-plained a lot.

"Well, shall we?" He took her hand, leading her into the circle of shells and pebbles the children had made on the smooth sand near the waves. He'd tried to memorise his lines, but it was all in vain. As he looked into her eyes, both hands linked, she took his breath away and with it his carefully prepared speech.

"Li Hua, I owe you so much, even my life. When you first came, and I saw you on the boat I thought I was crazy, that you were some sea goddess come from the deep, but now I know, you are an angel." For once there was no running translation, this was just for them. "I know you've been through so much, but it never touched your heart as it did mine. I promise from now on, I'll keep and protect you, and never let anyone hurt you again, ever. We'll work together to make a new and better world for the children, and I'll love and take care of you forever."

Her eyes were glowing with tears as she began, speeches forgotten, speaking in English for them alone.

"I feared you at first, but I came to see I could trust you. I watched how you played with the children, how you went with Hai to get the boat even though you weren't strong enough, how you forgave Jiao-long. You made me see not all men are bad, how I could come to trust a man ... I'm not scared anymore Vince. I want to be with you, look after you, work together and find healing together. I could never have loved a man other than you." Her tears were streaming now. Vince pulled her to him cradling her head on his shoulder. He was roughly awoken from his bliss as something hard pummelled his cheek. Li Hua squealed. The children were laughing, throwing something.

"What the ..."

"Rice. They're throwing rice," Li Hua shrieked. "It's the custom, but you don't throw it so close." She called to the children and the volley eased somewhat.

"Don't tell me, it's for good luck?" Vince ventured. She nodded.

Soon they were seated at the water's edge, the girls bringing plates of assorted fruit, rice and nuts. There was even a fish Hai had caught especially for the bride and groom. They were returning it seemed. There was a great deal of chattering going on, particularly aimed at Li Hua.

"What are they all on about?"

"They want to know what we said to each other mostly, and if I'm going to have a baby now."

"What did you tell them?"

"I said it was private between us, but I told them how we said we'd work together and care for each other and so on."

"What about the baby bit?"

"I said not everyone has babies. That they'll have to wait and see. Some of the girls are already fighting about who will take care of it." Vince smiled. One of the boys produced a handmade bamboo flute. As he played, Li Hua, and some of the children, joined in a strange and haunting song.

"It sounds so sad," Vince commented as it ended.

"It's a love song. Most old Chinese songs tend to be sad."

"Not anymore." He lent to kiss her forehead.

"Vince! It's beautiful! Beautiful! You did this for me?" Li Hua surveyed her new richly decorated abode.

"Well, the girls helped, and Hai of course. You said you liked bright colours?"

"I love it! Thankyou Vince!" she flung her arms around his neck, kissing him as she would a child. He kept his distance. Tonight would be hell he decided. Racoon, think racoon, he told himself. If he went too fast all could be lost. He had to let her make the moves in her own time. Pausing before the bedroom door, likewise adorned with scarlet and gold fabric, she entered, gasping and laughing for joy till her eyes alighted on the bed. Vince caught it instantly.

"If you prefer, we can ..."

"No Vince. I want to sleep with you, but ... but is it OK at first if we ..."

"I told you already Li Hua. We'll just sleep, that's all ... but look, maybe you should put on something a bit less alluring. I am a man after all." She giggled girlishly. "I'll er ... go for a walk on the beach ..." he stammered as he headed away from temptation.

The night air was cool and refreshing. He'd lain aside the waistcoat, but found the loose pants strangely comfortable, particularly for his aching loins. Hesitating for a moment, he plunged into the waves. It wasn't as cold as he'd hoped, but it did ease him a little. The boys were tittering on the shore, curiosity fuelling their interest. He could guess what they were saying, he'd been a boy once. Why were they still around? He should have got Li Hua to send them to bed, but he'd been too eager to show off his efforts with the cabin. He swam further along the beach seeking a little privacy to relieve himself ...

"You were gone a long time?" There she was, hair neatly braided, clad in her usual baggy T shirt, sheet pulled up. It was awkward.

"I went for a swim to cool down. It's hot in that waistcoat," he lied.

"Come, you must be tired." He slipped off the soaked pants retaining his boxers. Lying beside her, her head pillowed affectionately on his shoulder, he sought to sleep ...

She was gone when he woke but her smell still lingered, enticing. He got up quickly denying his mind any lingering thoughts How long could he keep this up, he wondered?

The following night was worse. He listened to her slow, steady breathing, curled, kitten like, on his shoulder, trusting, innocent of his hidden thoughts. He lay in dread of her waking to discover his aroused state, didn't want to scare her away when she'd come so close. He had feelings for her, more than the urge that throbbed in his groin, much more. She alone was party to his secret place, his vulnerability. He couldn't stand it if she shied away again. How long would it take to win her back? Easing her head onto the pillow he extricated himself bit by bit. Outside he breathed in the fresh sea air before slipping off into the greenery to "deal with business". It didn't take long.

On returning he was surprised to see her sitting up in bed, waiting.

"Where did you go, Vince?"

"I needed to pee," he lied. The moonlight streaming through the window hole caught her doubtful expression.

"You were gone a long time ..."

"I ..."

"Vince, don't lie to me. I know why you went, why you went swimming yesterday ... It's OK, I'm not mad at you."

"I thought it might ..."

"That it might scare me away? Look, I'm not a child. I'm stronger than you think. I trust you. I told you that. The very fact you creep away to relieve yourself strengthens that trust. But ... but I don't want you to do that anymore. It's not fair to ask it of you."

"You mean ..." his heart leapt.

"No, not that, not yet. It would bring back too many memories. I don't want to think of you that way."

"I don't want you to ... What are you suggesting?"

"That you don't need to go outside. I could ... help you."

"You mean you'd jack me off?" She set her finger to his lips.

"Don't use their language, Vince. It ..."

"Sorry, I didn't mean to ..."

"It's OK. It's just those kinds of words trigger things."

"Then we'll make our own words, our own lovemaking."

"Come." She patted the sheet beside her. "I need to erase some memories, build new ones in their place."

"Do I look like him? ... Was he a foreigner like me?" Vince stammered, the question slipping out. He'd worried it might be harder because he was a westerner. She nodded.

"He was a foreigner, but not like you. He was darker, more thickset, and even hairier.

"You don't like hair then?"

"Your hair is beautiful, the colour of sand, but the fur ... I don't like the fur so much. Our men have smooth skin, no hair."

He chuckled. "I could shave?"

"No, then you'd be all prickly, like your face." She rubbed her fingers on his stubbly cheek. "It doesn't feel nice." Fur! She thought of it like fur, like an animal! He felt insulted, but then she wasn't used to it. Chinese men after all were said to have very little body hair. She saw his disquiet and added. "Your eyes are beautiful though, like the sky or the sea. I guess the two go together. I just need to get used to you more ... Lie still. Promise you won't move?"

"What exactly do you have in mind?"

"I just want to get used to you." He was reminded of Brady, feeling used, dirty. This was altogether different. There was no coercion and her hands were gentle in their exploration. It was as if she were mapping his body, stroking, searching, following the natural curves and contours, her lips followed, tasting, probing, leaving touches, not of passion, but affection in their wake. He sighed. Passionate or not his body was beginning to react.

"Look Li Hua, there are some parts of my body I have no control over. I ..." He broke off as her hand slid down to encase him. Blood pulsed downward.

"You mean this part?" He could say nothing, shocked at her

158

sudden boldness. "Stay still, you promised. You're on trial, remember?" How could he forget? Her hands were both skilled and innocent, a blend of old and new. She giggled girlishly as she worked him, laughing that there were no tissues as he came, surging, in a pool on his belly. He pulled her down playfully against him.

"You made the mess, you must help clean it up," he joked. Then, unable to resist, he kissed her long and soundly, exploring the hidden recesses of her mouth. She pulled away. He let her go instantly.

"You got me all messy, besides you promised to keep still."

"I thought my ordeal was over."

"Ordeal? Is that what you call it?"

"The very best kind of ordeal." He wanted to kiss her again but didn't want to push his luck. "Let's go for a swim, get cleaned up." She nodded. He stopped her as she swung to gain her feet.

"You know I love you, Li Hua." He looked deep in her eyes.

"Yes, I know, I wouldn't trust you otherwise." She popped a quick kiss on his lips then darted out of the door chasing along the beach while Vince struggled to adjust his boxers. Catching her in the spray, he clasped her to him, waves crashing against them.

"I want you always and forever, Li Hua. Just don't ever leave me OK ... even if I am a furry animal to you." She laughed.

"Furry yes," she slid her hand down the soft curls that crossed his chest, "but never an animal." She raised her lips to his and they kissed long and deep. This time she did not pull back.

They were disturbed by a call from the beach. Hai stood calling at the brink of the waves.

"What's wrong?"

"He heard us making funny noises, then heard you calling me and running outside. He thought something was wrong. I told him we were just playing a game. He said he wants to play." She grinned.

Vince laughed, "I think we'd better change the game."

Calling him to come join them, he swung him round in the

surf, sitting him on his shoulders as they cased Li Hua through the surf. Hai had no idea what could have made Bohai so happy, but he was glad to be a part of it.

Slowly, slowly, like the rolling tides, like the sun rising over the sea, night after night they became more intimate, more at ease with each other till, one night, one glorious night, she straddled him taking him into herself. He lay inert, kissing, caressing, but not seeking to change position, rendering her total control. From there on passion grew between them, every night a feast of exploration. She no longer feared his advances, thrilled in his manliness. Partaking equally of loves delights, they, as she had said, created their own language of love and affection.

The boat tiller was finally fixed, huts grew along the beach, new innovations appeared from the reams of cloth – sarongs, simple, loose legged trousers, brilliant coloured skirts. Fish had returned, and one memorable day the spheres of light appeared once more, scattering the children, but bringing in their wake horses, a black and a chestnut, and their offspring.

Vince rode the waves, no longer alone, for Hai was at the tiller, hair wild in the wind, grinning at the haul of fish in their improvised net. Li Hua would be pleased. Her belly had yet to swell, but he knew the signs, her craving for fish was one of them. Vince wondered if she had partaken of Hai's healing, certainly it had been from that time on she'd let him touch her. Perhaps though it was part of a more general healing prevalent in nature itself. There had been no storms, none of the earthquakes common to the area Li Hua had spoken of, rice and crops grew well, untroubled by pests and diseases. Even in the growing tropical forests no mosquitos buzzed, or predators lurked, though animal life was returning.

Best of all the children were happy, their troubled past gradually eclipsed by the joys of life, of togetherness, though they would never forget those who died. Inspired by Vince's building efforts, Li Hua had conceived the idea of whittling crude figures or slabs with names engraved, to place in a flowery grove within the forest, a labour of love for each child to undertake. There Jiao-long's father found a place of rest, loved, forgiven, honoured. The children visited often to tell of some new project or happening. It was part of their culture, Li Hua explained, and a way of laying the past to rest so they could enter more fully into the present.

A new future dawned like the sun over the vast Pacific Ocean, uncharted, immense in possibilities, but not totally unknown. Every evening Vince read from the book that had been his only companion on his long voyage across the ocean. He read of troubled times and future promises and Li Hua translated for the children. They exchanged stories of the locust men, the blooded water, burning rocks from the sky, and the overwhelming quakes that changed their lives forever. Only Li Hua had been party to the sudden, agonising death of their oppressors, she said nothing of it. Suffice they knew that world was gone forever.